Zucchini
OUT
WEST

Zucchini OUT WEST

BARBARA DANA

ILLUSTRATIONS BY LYNETTE HEMMANT

HARPERCOLLINSPUBLISHERS

Acknowledgments
I would like to thank Dr. Tim W. Clark; Thomas M. Campbell III;
Dr. Tom Thorne; Jack Turnell; Lou Hanebury; Bob Oakleaf; Don Kwiatkowski;
and Bob Edgar. Without their help this book could not have been written.

Library of Congress Cataloging-in-Publication Data
Dana, Barbara.
  Zuchini out West / Barbara Dana ; illustrations by Lynette Hemmant.
    p.   cm.
  Summary: Ten-year-old Billy suspects that his pet ferret Zucchini may be a black-footed
ferret, one of the rarest mammals in the world, and takes him on a trip through the West to
meet the handful of black-footed ferrets known to exist.
  ISBN 0-06-024897-1. — ISBN 0-06-024898-X (lib. bdg.)
  [1. Black-footed ferret—Fiction.   2. Ferret—Fiction.   3. Pets—Fiction.
4. Endangered species—Fiction.   5. Rare animals—Fiction.   6. West (U.S.)—Fiction.
7. Voyages and travels—Fiction.]   I. Hemmant, Lynette, ill.   II. Title.
PZ7.D188Zw   1997   96-28976
[Fic]—dc20   CIP
                                                                                  AC

Typography by Al Cetta
1   2   3   4   5   6   7   8   9   10
❖
First Edition

To Molly

Emma's Mouse

ucchini had much to be thankful for. He loved his home, the fresh air and trees, the blue sky, the wind, the sounds of birds, his regular meals, his water bottle, and, most of all, Billy.

Billy is the most wonderful boy a ferret could have, Zucchini often thought.

Zucchini had recently come to live with Billy in Billy's new house in the country. Before that, he had lived in a cage at the ASPCA* on Ninety-second Street in New York City.

Zucchini never liked his cage at the ASPCA, or at the Bronx Zoo, where he was born, but at Billy's house it was different. He was locked inside only when Billy was at school. The rest of the time they would go on outings to Oppermans Pond, or to the meadow, or he would roam throughout the friendly house, curling up on the furniture, hiding under the slipcovers, and storing small things under the refrigerator.

Zucchini's cage was in the playroom. Billy closed the door at night but left Zucchini's cage open. That way Zucchini could go in and out whenever he wanted.

* Short for the American Society for the Prevention of Cruelty to Animals.

The playroom was full of boxes from the family's move that had not yet been unpacked. Pictures leaned against the wall, waiting to be hung. There were extra curtain rods, an ironing board, and a tennis racquet without strings. A plant gave the room a cozy feeling.

At night Zucchini was busy. He could climb on the boxes, sniff things, hide behind the pictures, curl up in the bookcase, creep around under the small couch, eat, drink, or play with his food bowl. He liked to pretend the bowl was another animal and attack it from behind. He would pounce on it, then grab it in his jaws and back up. Sometimes he would flip it over, then run from his cage and hide, but he only did this when the bowl was empty. His favorite thing was to sit in the window. Billy left the shade raised at night so Zucchini could watch the moonlight and listen for owls.

Before school Billy always fed Zucchini and gave him fresh water. Then he put Zucchini in his cage and pulled down the shade so Zucchini could sleep until he returned.

Billy had built the cage at school. It was large and made of wood and wire. It had a roomy main section with a smaller nest box inside. The nest box was made entirely of wood, with a small circle-shaped entryway. Inside the nest box it was dark and cozy. Billy had built the cage with great care. Zucchini could feel the love that Billy had put into it. It warmed him and made him feel at peace.

My life is good, Zucchini often thought. I have no cause to complain. There's just one small thing.

The small thing was small indeed, but it bothered Zucchini. It kept him awake. It irritated him and made him mad. The one small thing was Emma's mouse.

Emma was Billy's five-year-old sister, and Zucchini shared the playroom with her mouse. The mouse was white with a pink nose. Her tail was also pink, and so were her toes and the inside part of her ears. Her cage was kept across the room on a low table next to the window. It was smaller than Zucchini's cage and made of orange see-through plastic. Inside was a water bottle, a food bowl, a tumble of wood shavings, and a wheel. Constantly the mouse would tread the wheel, creaking her way to points unknown.

Squeak, squeak, rattle, rattle, bang, bang, went the wheel as the mouse ran feverishly, hour after hour, without a stop. Zucchini could get no rest.

Doesn't she ever sleep? he would wonder.

If the mouse wasn't on her wheel, she was chattering endlessly about stupid things, things that had no meaning. She rarely spoke to Zucchini. "Have to hurry," she would mumble. "No time. Lots of cheese." She would go on like that for hours, treading the wheel, repeating herself, making no sense.

Where on earth does she think she's going? Zucchini would wonder. What is in her pea-sized brain?

He tried to be understanding.

I shouldn't be bothered by such a tiny, helpless thing, he would think. So what if she runs on her wheel and she never sleeps and she talks to herself and she makes no sense? I have to ignore it. But how?

He didn't have an answer.

Billy

O ne Saturday morning, about three months after they had moved to the new house, there was a loud banging on the playroom door. It was Emma. "If you hear some banging on this door, it's me," she called. Then she opened the door and barged into the room. She wore a nightgown and carried a stuffed green stegosaurus. "Wake up, you guys," she said. "It's a shiny morning!"

Oh, no, thought Zucchini. Now this!

He was curled up inside his nest box, where he had just fallen asleep.

"Everybody up," said Emma. She made a sniffling noise with her nose, wrinkling up her face. "Don't mind my nose," she said. "I have a little cold, so I have to suck it in."

That's fine, thought Zucchini. Just do it in another room so I can sleep.

Emma stopped in front of the mouse's cage. She tapped on the orange plastic. This excited the mouse, who jumped onto her wheel and began to run, ears flat to her head.

Squeak, squeak, rattle, rattle, bang, bang.

Zucchini kept his eyes shut tight as if that might block out the sound of the wheel, but it didn't.

Emma dropped the stegosaurus on the floor. With both hands she removed the lid from the top of the mouse's cage. "Hello, One-Day Service," she said.

Zucchini had never understood the name. Emma's friend Myra had given Emma the mouse. They had been out in front of Myra's house at the time. Emma had quickly closed her eyes. "This mouse's name will be the first name I see," she had said. When she opened her eyes, there was the sign in the window of the dry cleaners across the street. "What does it say?" Emma had asked.

Myra was nine and could read. "One-Day Service," Myra had read.

At first Emma had wanted One-Day Service to be a male, but later she had changed her mind. "This mouse is a girl like me," she had decided. As it happened, this was the truth.

Emma reached into the cage and picked up the shivering mouse. "You are the smallest of small things," she said. "Want to ride in a truck?"

Emma loved trucks. She would often bring her dump truck into the playroom, put One-Day Service in the back, and push the truck around among the boxes and under the low table. She was allowed to do this only if the door to the playroom was closed. One time One-Day Service had gotten loose in the house and was nearly lost forever.

"Close the door."

It was Billy. He stood in the doorway in his pale-blue pajamas, not fully awake. He was thin with large eyes and light hair. Billy was ten years old and very shy, but his love of animals was strong. He understood them deeply and he loved Zucchini with all his heart.

Zucchini opened his eyes. He poked his head out through the small round opening of his wooden nest box to watch his friend.

"Close the door," repeated Billy. Whenever he spoke, you could see where one of his front teeth was chipped off at the corner. He had fallen on some stone steps when he was eight. Billy didn't like people asking about his tooth, especially other kids, who usually asked about it the first minute they met him.

Billy moved further into the room. "Close the door," he said.

"I'm holding my mouse," said Emma.

"That's why you have to close the door."

"I don't have hands," said Emma.

"Yes you do."

"It's an obstacle illusion."

"Optical illusion," said Billy. "And you do have hands."

"They're used."

Zucchini came out of his nest box and sat near the front of his cage, watching Billy with bright and steady eyes.

"Mom doesn't want One-Day loose in the house," said Billy.

"Her name is One-Day Service," said Emma. "That's her whole and real name and you have to use it."

"No I don't," said Billy.

Emma sat down suddenly on the floor. She held One-Day Service in her hands, clasped just beneath her chin.

Billy closed the door. "Mice don't like to be held that way," he said. "You have to let them breathe."

"She's breathing."

"I don't see how."

"In and out," said Emma. She made deep breathing noises and puffed up her chest.

"I know how to breathe," said Billy. "Loosen your hands so she can get some air."

Emma loosened her hands.

"Why don't you watch cartoons till Mom and Dad get up?"

"O.K.," said Emma. She got up, put One-Day Service back in her cage, picked up her stegosaurus, and headed into the living room to watch TV.

Billy moved to Zucchini's cage. Zucchini stood up and stretched, nose downward, happy to be close to his friend. Billy opened the door of the cage, reached his hand in, and stroked Zucchini along his back.

"You need some quiet," said Billy. He knew the mouse was noisy. He wished Zucchini's cage could be kept in his room, but his mother felt the playroom was best. He picked up Zucchini and carried him into his room. He set Zucchini down on the bed. "Rest now," he said.

Thank you, thought Zucchini. He curled up gratefully on the soft comforter and went to sleep.

Potbellied Pig

t breakfast Emma was excited about a package that was waiting for her at the post office. "So when do we get my present?" she asked. She was pouring maple syrup onto her

waffle, filling up the tiny squares, then letting the syrup run over the sides of the waffle.

"That's enough syrup!" said Mrs. Ferguson. She wore a large work shirt and jeans.

"All the squares have to be filled so they don't get lonesome."

"They're not going to get lonesome," said Billy. He was sitting on the floor by the kitchen closet organizing newspapers and paper bags, tying them into separate stacks. Saturday was recycling day and it was Billy's job. He cared a lot about ecology. The thought that so many animals were disappearing forever was a worry to him. He also worried about the trees that were being cut down, trees that were needed so that everyone could breathe. He worried about the pollution of the oceans and lakes and rivers and how the fish were getting poisoned. He worried about the bad air in the cities from all the cars and factories, and how holes were getting burned in the atmosphere and harmful rays of the sun were coming through. He worried about the waste from chemicals being buried in the ground.

Mr. Ferguson wished Billy wouldn't worry so much about those things. He said Billy should spend more time playing sports and making friends, but Billy couldn't help being worried.

"So when do we get my present?" Emma asked.

"It's not necessarily a present," said Mr. Ferguson, looking over the top of his newspaper. He was Billy and Emma's stepfather. Their parents had been divorced for two years. Their real father was an actor in Los Angeles, California.

"It said on the paper that Mom has that's yellow," said

Emma. Maple syrup ran down her chin and onto her night-gown. "It's a present for me!"

"It said package," said Billy, tying up a tall stack of papers with twine.

"I hope it's a potbellied pig," said Emma.

"It's not," said Billy.

"How do you know?"

"You can count on it."

"I can't count," said Emma. She took a long sip of juice through her twisted orange straw from Busch Gardens. "It might be a pig," she added. "It might be there right now in a big box with boarded-up nails, waiting for me and hungry."

"They don't send pigs to the post office," said Billy.

"Where do they send them?"

"To the airport, or they deliver them in a truck."

Emma ran to the window and peered out. "There's no truck," she said.

"There's no pig," said Billy.

"Have your breakfast, Bill," said Mr. Ferguson.

Billy got up, leaving the partially stacked papers and twine and scissors on the floor. He didn't like it when his stepfather called him Bill. It made him feel as if his stepfather wanted him to be more grown up than he was. He sat down at the table as Emma returned from the window. "I hope it's a potbellied pig," she said. "You can tie a neck scarf on them like a cowgirl would have and they never mind."

"We can't have a pig," Mrs. Ferguson said firmly.

"Why not?"

"There's enough to do without pigs."

"Just one."

"No." Mrs. Ferguson illustrated children's books. She had a busy life and often said that two pets were all they could care for.

"They're dry and cute," said Emma.

"What is?" asked Mr. Ferguson.

"A potbellied pig," said Emma. "They're dry and cute, like a bowling ball would be with hair on it."

"We can't have a pig now," said Mrs. Ferguson. Something in her tone told Emma there was no further point in asking.

Zucchini's Dream

s Billy and Emma and Mr. Ferguson began their Saturday errands, Zucchini was having a dream. He dreamed of light and air and open spaces. It was a dream he had quite often. In the dream he was out on a prairie in the clear, bright sun. The ground stretched out for miles, with pale-green bushes and lavender wildflowers. Tall mountains rose in the distance. He was running, feeling the sun on his face, the wind rushing by, happy and free. He felt no edges to his body. He was part of the air and the mountains and the flowers. He knew he could fly if he wanted to, but he didn't need to. He was flying already inside.

Suddenly, One-Day Service appeared. She was gigantic in size and carried an enormous piece of cheese. She chattered loudly, but the strange thing was she didn't open her mouth. This made Zucchini nervous. The feeling of being able to fly went away, and so did the feeling of being a part of nature.

"Everybody needs cheese," said the mouse, mouth closed, growing larger as she spoke. She was blocking Zucchini's way. Although he could have gone around her, he felt unable to move.

"I don't need cheese," said Zucchini. "I don't even like cheese."

"Everybody needs cheese," repeated the mouse, mouth shut tight.

"Let me pass," said Zucchini.

One-Day Service was towering over Zucchini. She opened her mouth and the enormous cheese began to fall, straight down toward Zucchini.

Cheese coming! he thought. Help! I'll be squashed!

Before the cheese could reach Zucchini, he woke up, his heart pounding in his chest. He was safe in Billy's room.

Thank goodness! he thought. It was only a dream!

Then he fell into a deep sleep.

As Zucchini slept, Billy and Emma and Mr. Ferguson drove along the country road toward the post office. The family lived just outside Binghamton, New York, where Mr. Ferguson ran an audio equipment store. The car moved along, past Oppermans Pond, where Billy often took Zucchini for walks. The pond was set in a pine forest.

"I wonder," said Emma. She was in the backseat, holding

her stuffed stegosaurus and a small bag of chips her mother had given her for a snack. Billy thought she might say more, but she didn't.

"What do you wonder?" asked Mr. Ferguson.

"Who could have sent me the pig?"

"No one," said Billy.

"Michael Maloney maybe did. He's my really better friend. His brother can shake his eyeballs."

"My goodness," said Mr. Ferguson.

"Can you beat it?" said Emma.

Mr. Ferguson rolled down the window. He breathed in the early-spring air. "Baseball season's coming," he said. Mr. Ferguson loved sports, especially baseball. He was always trying to get Billy to play, but Billy wasn't very good in sports. The other kids took sports so seriously. Billy always felt he would spoil the game for them, or they would laugh. The more he worried about these things, the harder it was for him to play. Mr. Ferguson thought sports would be good for Billy. He thought it would help his shyness. Billy didn't know if that was true, but even if it was, he figured he'd help his shyness some other way.

"We have to catch the Phillies this year," continued Mr. Ferguson.

"Who threw them?" asked Emma.

"Nobody threw them," said Billy.

"I want to take Billy to see them," said Mr. Ferguson. "What do you say, Bill?"

"O.K.," said Billy. He didn't want to hurt his stepfather's feelings by telling him he didn't want to go.

Inside the small post office several people were lined up in front of the counter.

Emma burst through the door. "Have you got a potbellied pig around here?" she asked.

The post-office clerk, a serious-looking woman with a ring of keys at her belt, looked up from where she was weighing a package. "You'll have to wait your turn," she said.

Mr. Ferguson handed Emma the slip. "Get in line," he said.

Billy was disappointed to see the line of people waiting. He was eager to get to the recycling station and back to Zucchini.

When it was Emma's turn, she reached up and handed the yellow slip to the clerk. The clerk took the slip, then disappeared behind a partition. She reappeared almost immediately with a medium-sized rectangular box wrapped in brown paper. "Here you go," she said. She handed the box to Emma, who took it, moving away from the counter to a spot near the door. There she stood, clutching the package, tears welling up in her eyes. Her lower lip began to tremble.

"Let's see what it is," said Mr. Ferguson.

Emma began to cry. "There's no room," she said.

"Open it," said Mr. Ferguson.

"There's no room for a pig."

"Want me to help you?" asked Billy.

"I can do it," said Emma. Tears flowing, she took the package, sat down on the floor, pulled off the paper, and opened the box. Inside was a furry kangaroo suit, just her size.

Recycling

Zucchini was just waking up. He stretched in the bright ray of sunshine that slanted in through the window. Then he stood up on the comforter, shook himself, and looked about the room. Pictures of animals covered every wall.

Above Billy's bed was a poster of a timber wolf standing on a rock in the Alaskan wilderness. At first Zucchini had found the wolf a bit scary, but he had gotten used to it. He liked the stillness of the snow.

At the side of Billy's desk hung a long strip of paper with a list of all the endangered and threatened species in the world. The strip was taller than Billy, with small print on both sides. Zucchini knew it was Billy's dream to help shorten that list. He had heard Billy say he wanted to help save the lives of the animals on the list, but he didn't know how he was going to do it.

Zucchini jumped down off the bed and hurried to the window. He jumped onto the windowsill, looking out at the clear, cool day. Two crows circled excitedly just beyond the oak tree. They cawed to each other, trading bits of information, good news of some sort. He watched until they flew off in search of food.

I'm hungry, he thought.

Then he remembered.

My food is in my cage. My cage in the playroom.

One-Day Service is in the playroom. She'll be running on her wheel. She'll tell me about cheese. I'd rather stay here.

As they pulled up to the recycling station, Emma was playing with the stuffed baby kangaroo in her pouch. Only Emma's face showed from inside the fuzzy suit. The costume was a present from an actor friend of her father's who was making a film in Australia.

Billy got out of the car, went around to the trunk, opened it, and picked up one of the blue carrying crates filled with glass and plastic containers. Mr. Ferguson joined him, picking up two stacks of papers, then following him up the wooden stairs to the platform. Large garbage Dumpsters lined each side. GLASS AND PLASTIC, said the sign on one of the Dumpsters; CANS, said another; PAPER, said the next.

The recycling coordinator stood on the platform. He knew Billy well. "Hello, Billy," he said.

"Hello," said Billy.

"You never miss a Saturday," said the recycling coordinator.

"No," said Billy. He wanted to say more. He wanted to say, "Glad to see you, Mr. Nordman. Thanks for letting me help last week," but he couldn't. He was too shy. He dumped the glass and plastic containers into the appropriate Dumpster. Then he went back down the stairs to get another crate.

Emma was coming up the stairs in her kangaroo suit, carrying three aluminum cans. "Kangaroos like to carry cans," she said.

"A kangaroo recycling garbage," said Mr. Nordman. "I've seen everything."

"Maybe not," said Emma.

"Do you take these?" A small, dark-haired woman put the question to Mr. Nordman. She carried a broken toaster.

"Sorry, no," said Mr. Nordman.

The woman looked confused. Billy headed up the stairs with his last load as she turned to leave. He wondered why she was so upset. Did she love the toaster? Was she afraid of putting it in the wrong place? He knew what it was like to worry about little things. It was happening to him now. There was a recycling drive next week. Billy wanted to ask Mr. Nordman if he could help, but he didn't have the nerve.

I'd probably be in the way, he thought as he dumped the cans into the Dumpster.

As he turned to leave, Mr. Nordman waved good-bye. "There's a drive next week," he called. "Hope you can help."

Black-Footed Ferret

hen Billy got home, the first thing he did was to bring Zucchini a bowl of food.

Thank you! thought Zucchini.

He jumped off the windowsill and began to eat, his tiny teeth breaking up the kibbles of dry food. Billy lay down on the bed to watch him. Zucchini's yellow-buff fur shone in the sunlight that streamed in through the window.

Zucchini was nineteen inches long, with a five-inch black-tipped tail. He weighed about two pounds. Although he was only six months old, he was already full grown, as ferrets mature quickly. He had a long, thin body with short legs, a long neck, and short, rounded ears.

Billy had read a lot about ferrets. He knew they were members of a group of weasellike mammals known as mustelids. He knew there were different kinds of ferrets. There was the domestic or European ferret, the kind sold in pet stores, and there was the black-footed ferret, one of the rarest mammals in the world. There was also the Siberian ferret, which resembled a black-footed ferret but wasn't.

Zucchini looked up suddenly from his food bowl. He stared at Billy with bright eyes.

Billy loved Zucchini's black face mask, his pale-tipped ears, his shiny black nose set in a circle of near-white fur.

Could you be a black-footed ferret? he wondered.

The woman who ran the children's zoo at the ASPCA had said he was. Her name was Miss Pickett and she knew a lot about animals. She said black-footed ferrets were endangered. She said they lived out west. She said it would be unusual to find one on Ninety-second street. Zucchini looked like a black-footed ferret, she said. She would do some research to make sure.

Billy got up and went over to his desk. He picked up his favorite issue of *Defenders of Wildlife*, the one with the black-footed ferret on the cover. He had studied the picture many times. He liked to compare it to Zucchini. Both had the same dark, bright eyes, the same black face mask, the same black feet and black-tipped tail.

"Look at this," said Billy, sitting down next to Zucchini. The ferret on the cover was perched halfway out of a prairie-dog burrow, its front paws on the ground, its rear half below. With sharp eyes it stared into the distance, still and watching. The great expanse of prairie stretched out in all directions.

How beautiful, thought Zucchini. It looks like my dream.

A dog barked. It was Sonya, the German shepherd who lived next door. She was barking at the short woman in men's slacks who had come to read the gas meter.

Zucchini stood suddenly on his hind legs, tall, alert, completely still. He looked exactly like the picture.

You can't be a black-footed ferret, Billy thought. It's against the law to keep endangered animals. Miss Pickett knows that. Why would she have let me keep you?

He thought of writing her a letter, but he decided against it.

She wouldn't remember me, he reasoned. Maybe she didn't say you were a black-footed ferret anyway. I must have heard her wrong.

Tim Clark

illy opened the top left-hand drawer of his desk, reached in, and took out a small wooden box. It was a present Billy's father had brought him from Spain. The lid was hand

carved and showed a medieval soldier on horseback. The horse had a long mane and the soldier carried a spear. It was the most precious thing Billy owned.

Zucchini jumped onto Billy's desk.

Nice box, he thought.

Inside the box Billy kept his most valuable belongings: a shark's tooth; an ancient coin from Mexico; a tiny black pocketknife his stepfather had given him; a picture of himself holding Zucchini at the ASPCA; his National Audubon Society membership card; three purple marbles; and most important of all, his letter from Tim Clark.

Tim Clark was a hero of Billy's. He was a professor at Yale University who was an expert on mammal ecology and behavior. Dr. Clark had researched many mammals, but the black-footed ferret was his favorite. He had spent years searching for the animal, studying its habits, and gathering information that could help the survival of the species.

Billy had written Dr. Clark a letter as part of a report he was doing at school. The assignment went like this:

Career Report
1. *Choose a person whose work you admire.*
2. *Tell what problems you would face in his or her line of work.*
3. *Tell what you think would be the rewards.*
4. *Write this person a letter asking at least two questions. (If he or she writes back, include the answers in your report.)*

It had taken Billy days to get up the courage to write his letter. When the answer came, he could hardly believe it.

Zucchini watched as Billy sat down in the chair at his desk, opened the box, and took out the letter.

Dear Billy,

　　Thank you for your letter.

　　I am pleased to learn of your interest in the black-footed ferret.

　　I enclose the answers to your questions. I hope they will be of help to you in completing your report.

　　Best of luck to you.

Long live ferrets,
Tim Clark

On a separate page were the answers to Billy's questions, written in Dr. Clark's own hand. Tim Clark had actually written to him! He could hardly believe it. Billy folded the letter carefully, then returned it to the box. He was going to keep this letter forever.

Phone Call

t lunchtime the phone rang. It was Billy's father calling from Florida, where he was making a movie.

"It's your father," said Mrs. Ferguson.

"I have to go to the bathroom," said Emma. She sat on a

high kitchen stool, wearing her kangaroo suit and eating french fries. She was still mad at her father for leaving and wouldn't talk to him when he called. She climbed down off the stool and headed for the hall. "Get me out of this kangaroo," she said. She hurried into the bathroom and closed the door.

Zucchini was curled up next to the phone. He watched as Billy sat down and picked up the receiver. "Hello," said Billy.

"Ready for spring vacation?" asked his dad.

"Sure," Billy answered.

Billy missed his father a lot. He and Emma spent their school vacations with him. Often they would travel to different movie locations to visit. They had been to Mexico, Los Angeles, Canada, and Alabama. Billy enjoyed his time on movie sets. The crew was friendly and often taught him rope tricks.

"Where would you like to go?" his father asked.

"I don't know," said Billy.

"Think about it. We'll go somewhere fun."

"O.K.," said Billy.

While Billy was talking, Mrs. Ferguson tried to get Emma to come out of the bathroom. "Daddy wants to talk to you," she called through the closed door.

"I'm not available," said Emma. "You'll have to take a message."

After Billy hung up the phone, he went to the refrigerator to get some milk. Zucchini watched as Billy took out the milk, closed the refrigerator door, and returned to the table.

"What time is it when the elephant sits on the fence?" asked Emma. She came into the kitchen, zipping her kangaroo suit up the front. "Give up?" she added.

"I give up," said Mr. Ferguson.

"Time to get a new elephant."

"A new fence," said Billy. "You always tell it wrong."

"It's my joke," said Emma.

"It's everybody's joke," said Billy.

"So I can tell it how I want."

"What are your vacation plans?" asked Mr. Ferguson, biting into the second half of his cheese sandwich.

"I don't know," said Billy. He didn't like to talk to his stepfather about his father. Although he loved his stepfather, he felt a special closeness with his father. He worried that his stepfather would sense this, that it would hurt his feelings.

"Will your father be picking you up?" asked Mr. Ferguson.

"If his shooting doesn't run over."

"Like a bath?" asked Emma.

"No," said Billy.

Emma dipped a french fry into the ketchup and popped it into her mouth.

That night Billy lay in bed, his mind full of plans. There were so many places he could go with his father. They would have to take Emma, of course, but they would have fun anyway. Times with his dad were special. There were always surprises. With his stepfather it was different. He liked to eat at the same time every day and sit in the same chair and read his electronic-equipment magazines and listen to classical music and go to ball games and fix things around the house. Billy's father liked to leave dishes in the sink sometimes and go out driving at midnight and go to the movies on weekday afternoons and wear shoes without socks. Once they had pizza for breakfast.

Where will we go? thought Billy as he lay awake, the covers pulled up to his chin. We could go fishing, or camping, or climb the Adirondacks. Dad could carry Emma.

Billy's mind raced with ideas of the wonderful places they could go. Then all at once a thought struck him.

Zucchini! I can't leave him! How can I go?

Hopeless

That same night Zucchini had a talk with One-Day Service. He watched from the windowsill as she ran on her wheel. She had been running for hours and Zucchini needed some peace. He moved to the edge of her cage. After a moment, he spoke. "Where are you going?" he asked.

"Places," said the mouse, picking up speed. Her tiny paws moved too quickly, almost, to be seen.

"What kind of places?" asked Zucchini.

"No time," said the mouse.

"You're in a cage."

"I know that," said the mouse.

"What are your options?"

"My options?"

"Your choices?"

"No time," said the mouse.

"I could open your cage," said Zucchini. "I let a crow out once. He went to Staten Island."

There was no response from the mouse. Ears flat to her head, she ran, staring straight through the orange plastic of her cage at the wall on the far side of the room.

"There are wonderful places," Zucchini continued. "You could go to the prairie. You could go to the woods."

"I like it here," said the mouse.

"Then why do you keep running on your wheel?"

"Don't be late," said the mouse.

"Late for what?"

"You never know."

Zucchini sat down. "Let me get this straight," he said. "You're hurrying to get you don't know where, so you don't miss you don't know what. Is that what you're saying?"

"Pretty much," said the mouse.

"I don't understand."

"You never know what you're missing."

"You're missing what's here!" said Zucchini. "You've got a den, you've got food, you've got a family that loves you."

"Have to hurry. Lots of cheese."

"Emma gives you cheese."

"There's always more," said the mouse.

"Enjoy the cheese you have."

"Have to hurry. No time. Lots of cheese."

Zucchini turned and looked out through the window at the moon, a large white circle high above the oak tree in the yard.

It's hopeless, he thought. I'll never understand her.

Painting

illy had planned to take Zucchini to Oppermans Pond on Sunday, but it rained, a heavy, freezing March rain, and they had to stay inside. In the morning Billy and his mother painted furniture. Mr. Ferguson had taken Emma to the library, so Billy and his mother were working by themselves.

Billy was quiet. He was often quiet, but this was different, not a comfortable, everything-is-in-order kind of quiet, but a silence, heavy with concern. Billy's mother wondered about it, but she didn't say anything.

Billy had two things on his mind. First there was the vacation.

What will I do? he wondered as he stirred the paint with the wooden mixing stick from the paint store. I want to go with Dad, but I can't leave Zucchini. He wouldn't understand.

He was also worried about his report. He had to turn it in tomorrow and it wasn't finished. He wanted it to be good, and now he couldn't concentrate.

"Is something wrong?" Mrs. Ferguson asked at last.

"I'm O.K.," said Billy. He didn't like to make a big thing about his feelings.

After lunch Billy took Zucchini into his room and closed

the door. He sat on the edge of the bed holding Zucchini close. "I don't want to leave you," he said.

Leave me? thought Zucchini. Panic shot through his tiny body like a knife.

"I can't," said Billy.

Thank goodness, thought Zucchini. What would I do without you?

"I love you," Billy said quietly.

I love you too, thought Zucchini.

Billy got up and set Zucchini down on the floor next to his favorite toy. Billy had made it from a plastic gallon water jug that Mr. Ferguson had bought at the market. When the family finished the water, Billy cut several ferret-sized holes in the plastic, making it into a kind of playhouse. Zucchini loved it. He would climb in and out, hide inside, or sit, peering out the top hole, watching things and feeling cozy.

"Play in your jug," said Billy when he set him down.

Zucchini climbed in through one of the holes in the side, turned around several times within the den of plastic, then popped his head out the top and stared at Billy.

Don't ever leave me, he thought. You're my truest friend.

Billy lay down on his bed and opened his blue loose-leaf notebook. He had to finish his report. He stared at the first page, but he couldn't concentrate. Thoughts of leaving Zucchini filled his mind.

Just then Emma opened the door. She wore her kangaroo suit and carried her stuffed stegosaurus. "What do you think?" she asked.

"I can't talk now," said Billy.

Emma sat on the bed. "Dad's in the basement and I'm

doing stickers and coloring. Do you get the picture?"

"I'm working," said Billy.

"Suddenly, right off the bat, I hear him and guess what?"

"Who said you could come in here?" Billy asked.

"There's mice!"

Mice? thought Zucchini.

"Can you beat it?" asked Emma.

Billy looked up from his notebook.

"I'm telling you," said Emma. "The ones that squeak, with tails and teeny feet?"

"I know what they are," said Billy.

That's all we need, thought Zucchini.

Emma sat cross-legged on the comforter. She held her stegosaurus tight. "I go in and suddenly, right off the bat, I see Dad in the basement and he's holding a Cross-Your-Heart trap."

"Have-a-Heart," said Billy.

"I know," said Emma. "It's this trap that's metal with shutting end doors, and you put food inside like peanut butter or maybe cheese, but it doesn't have a squashing bar to squash the mouse, just the shutting doors, and so the mouse heads for the food, and this thing goes pop, and the end doors shut, *bang*, and the mouse is trapped and scared, but it isn't hurt."

"I know how they work," said Billy.

"There's a mouse!" said Emma. "I'm telling you. It's brown and shaking with pop-out eyes."

Zucchini pulled his head back in through the hole in his plastic jug.

"Want to see it?" asked Emma.

Billy set down his notebook. "O.K.," he said, "but then I have to work."

"You have to look fast because we're taking it to Gedney Park."

Good! thought Zucchini.

"It has to be far enough so it doesn't know the way back, but close enough so I can visit," Emma continued.

"You'll never find it," said Billy.

"I have my ways," said Emma. She climbed down off the bed. "I'll bring some cheese and then I'll use a certain calling voice and the mouse will know it's me with cheese. We can play in the park, or I can bring it home for parties."

"What parties?"

"Different ones. I have it planned."

"It won't work," said Billy.

Let's hope not, thought Zucchini.

School

illy's teacher was interested in ecology. Her name was Ms. Crystal and Billy liked her a lot. The first project after he arrived at the new school in January was to make the room look like a jungle in Brazil. They studied the rain forest. They painted murals of many of the plants and animals to be found there. Trees painted on heavy brown paper surrounded the class. Vines hung like streamers from the ceiling. Parrots and toucans were painted on the windows. A mural of a waterfall covered the wall behind Ms. Crystal's desk.

Billy loved the room. He found it comforting to read, or write, or work on math, surrounded by the animals and the foliage, listening to the *Sounds of the Jungle* tape Ms. Crystal often played.

Ms. Crystal was concerned about the destruction of the rain forest. She said trees were needed to help sustain the lives of all the creatures on the earth. The class was planning an Earth Day Fair to raise money to buy some of the rain forest. They wanted to save what little part of it they could.

The day Billy's report was due, Ms. Crystal made an announcement. She stood in front of her desk, her long brown hair pulled back with a silver clasp. "Before you hand in your reports, I'd like you to read them aloud," she said.

Billy's heart pounded in his chest.

I can't do that! he thought.

"Some of you will read your reports today and some tomorrow," Ms. Crystal continued.

Let my turn be tomorrow! thought Billy. I'll stay home!

"The students on the left side of the room will read their reports today."

Billy's heart skipped a beat. His desk was on the left!

Oh, no! he thought. I'll mess it up. They'll laugh at me. They'll think I'm dumb.

"Kristen is first," Ms. Crystal continued.

Kristen was blond and tidy. Stopping in front of Ms. Crystal's desk, she clasped her hands in front of her gray wool skirt. "My report is on my aunt, Stephanie Notion," she began.

"Ms. Notion is an assistant buyer for the May Company department store."

Billy's heart was racing now. His hands were cold. Two other students followed. Mike's report was on the baseball player Cal Ripken. Kenneth told about his father, who sold insurance.

When Billy was called, he felt hot and cold all at once. When he stood up, his knees felt weak. Holding his report, he moved to the front of the class. His heart was pounding. His shirt was wet under the arms because he was sweating already. He turned to face the class. Instead of looking into the faces of his classmates, he looked straight to the back of the room at the mural on the rear wall. It showed an alligator dozing in a swamp, eyes bulging beneath closed lids. Billy swallowed, then looked down and began to read. "My report is on Tim Clark," he read. His voice was small and hard to hear. "Tim Clark is a doctor of zoology. One of the things he does is look for animals that are getting extinct. He studies their habits and he thinks up ways to save them."

"I can't hear you," said Bruce. He sat near the windows, drawing pictures of explosions on the cover of his notebook.

"Can you speak louder, Billy?" Ms. Crystal asked. "Your subject is fascinating. I want us all to hear."

Billy tried to clear his throat. It felt like his voice was trapped inside.

I can't do this, he thought.

He forced himself to continue. That was when he mixed up some of the words. He said "engainjured" instead of endangered and "peachees" instead of species. Several kids laughed when he said that. He wished he could disappear.

"One animal Dr. Clark studied for many years was the black-footed ferret," Billy continued. "They live on prairie dogs. A lot of ranchers poison prairie dogs because they don't want them to eat their grass and make holes. When the prairie dogs are poisoned, the ferrets have no food, so they die."

Billy tried to take a deep breath, but he couldn't relax enough to get much air. "Tim Clark didn't see any ferrets for eight years," he continued, "but he kept looking. Other biologists looked too. Finally they found ninety ferrets in Wyoming. They took pictures and made maps."

Billy's heart still pounded, but at least he wasn't getting the words mixed up anymore and no one said they couldn't hear.

"In a few years the ferrets began to disappear," Billy went on. "Dr. Clark said they should take some ferrets into captivity. Some people thought this was a good idea, but some people didn't. Soon there were only fourteen ferrets left. They took six ferrets into captivity, but they died."

At this point Billy noticed the class was quiet. A few kids looked bored, but the others seemed to be listening. He kept going. "When they looked again, there were only six ferrets in the wild. They took them to a building and kept them in different rooms so they all wouldn't catch a bad disease if one of the ferrets had it. Dr. Clark said they should breed the ferrets. He said when new babies came and grew up, they should put some back on the prairie. That's what they're doing now."

Ms. Crystal was smiling. This made Billy feel a little better. He read Dr. Clark's letter, the questions he had asked, and the answers Dr. Clark had given. "Question number one,"

Billy read. " 'Do you think there are any more black-footed ferrets in the wild that we don't know about?' Answer: 'Some days I think there might be, other days not.' Question number two: 'Do you think black-footed ferrets can be saved?' Answer: 'The chances are good, but it will take many years.' "

I'm almost finished! Billy thought.

"I admire Tim Clark's work," he read, "because I think it's important to save the earth and all the animals before it's too late. I would like to follow in his footsteps because I love animals and I want to help save them. It would be hard because people have almost ruined the earth, so it's a big job to fix it. It would be rewarding because I would be doing something to save the animals and all of nature so we can go on living. The end."

Billy looked up from his report. He stared at the alligator dozing in the swamp and the toucan in the tree. The class was quiet.

Lima Beans

When school was over, Ms. Crystal stopped Billy on his way out. "Your report was excellent," she said.

"I messed it up," said Billy.

"No, you didn't." Ms. Crystal was at her desk, putting

papers into her large purple woven bag. "You have a wonderful feeling for your subject."

"Thank you," said Billy. He was glad she'd liked it, even if the kids hadn't. He could still hear their laughter when he had mixed up the words, their silence when he had finished.

Ms. Crystal picked up her keys, along with a small plastic bottle of carrot juice. "Have you always been interested in conservation?" she asked.

"Yes," said Billy.

"We need people like you."

"Thanks," said Billy.

"You're welcome," said Ms. Crystal. "The planet could use some help."

When Billy got home from school, his mother was in her studio room working on some sketches. She gave Billy a hug and asked how things had gone at school.

"I messed up my report," Billy told her.

"How?" his mother asked.

"We had to read them and I couldn't talk loud enough and I mixed up the words and the kids laughed. They thought it was stupid."

"I doubt that," his mother said. "A few kids may have laughed, but that doesn't mean they thought it was stupid. What did your teacher say?"

"She said it was good."

"There, you see," said his mother. "I'll bet it was good."

"It was a good report," said Billy, "but I stank it up when I read it."

"I'm sure it went better than you think," his mother said. "I made you some cookies."

"Thanks," said Billy. Then he left the room.

A little later Billy sat at the kitchen table holding Zucchini and eating the ginger cookies his mother had made. A breeze blew in through the open window above the sink, moving the yellow curtains.

This is nice, thought Zucchini. I wish it could always be like this, without One-Day Service making a racket all the time. I have to do something about that mouse.

When Billy finished the cookies, he picked up Zucchini and went to the refrigerator to see if there were any leftover lima beans. Billy didn't like lima beans, but Zucchini did, especially the soft centers. He stored the skins under the living-room couch.

Billy's mother came into the kitchen. She told Billy she had to pick Emma up at ballet class. "Feel better?" she asked.

"I guess so," said Billy.

"I'll be back in half an hour," his mother said. Then she left.

Billy opened the refrigerator. On the top shelf was a bowl of lima beans. He opened the plastic lid and took out a lima bean.

Lima beans! thought Zucchini. My favorite!

Zucchini took the bean gently from Billy's fingers, chewed, then spit the skin on the floor.

The phone rang. It was Billy's father calling from the movie set in Florida. When Billy told him about his report and how the kids had laughed, his father said, "So what?" Billy's father was like that. He was blunt and honest and not at all interested in what other people thought. "Next time talk louder," he added.

"I can't," said Billy.

"Sure you can," said his father. "It's scary talking in front of people. You have to get used to it. Listen, I have a great idea. Are you ready?"

"Yes," said Billy.

"We're going to Wyoming."

"Wyoming?"

"We'll see the ferrets. Like you said in your report. We'll see where they breed them. We'll talk to the biologists. We'll hike in the Tetons. They have the Tetons over there."

"I know," said Billy.

"We'll take an extra week. Make it two. Ask Mom to talk to the school."

"O.K.," said Billy.

"It's educational," his father added. "Anyway, I haven't seen you in months. We need some time."

Billy was excited. A chance to see the prairies, to meet the biologists, to see the only black-footed ferrets in the world, the ones that looked like Zucchini.

Zucchini!

"So what do you say?" Billy's father asked.

Billy was quiet.

"Are you there?"

"I can't go," said Billy.

"What?" his father asked.

"I can't go."

"What do you mean?"

"I can't leave Zucchini."

Oppermans Pond

"**W**e'll take him," said Billy's father.

Billy's heart raced with excitement. "Could we do that?"

"Why not? We're driving. It's perfect."

"That's great!"

"I have to go," said Billy's father. "They need me for a shot."

"O.K.," said Billy.

"See if it's all right with Mom and ask her to talk to the school."

"I will."

"I love you," said his father. And he hung up.

Billy put the receiver back down on the hook. For a moment he was unable to move. He could hardly believe it was true. A trip to Wyoming! And he could take Zucchini! He wished his mother was there so he could tell her the news. He was pretty sure she would let him go. She would know how much the trip meant to him. She had to say yes!

Zucchini stared at Billy with bright and questioning eyes. He could sense Billy's excitement.

"We're going to the pond," said Billy. "I have something to tell you."

What is it? thought Zucchini.

"I want to tell you at our special place."

Billy gave Zucchini a final lima bean. Then he set him down. He moved to the phone table and wrote his mother a note.

> Gone to Oppermans Pond.
> Took Zucchini. Back soon.
>   Billy

Zucchini followed Billy into his room and watched as Billy put on his blue sweatshirt with the hood. Billy had taught Zucchini to ride in the hood as it hung down his back. There was nothing Zucchini liked more than to curl up there and watch the sights as Billy hiked along the road past his house and down the dirt path toward Oppermans Pond.

The sun was low in the sky as they set out. The breeze was strong. The oak tree stood firm in the yard, but the smaller trees bent in the wind. In the meadow to the right, just past Billy's house, a group of Canada geese selected blades of grass near the side of the road. Unhurried, they searched, necks curved, beaks to the ground. A woodpecker tapped at the trunk of the dead tree at the edge of the pine woods.

What will he tell me? thought Zucchini. Maybe One-Day Service is going to live with a friend. Maybe she's going to visit the other mouse at Gedney Park. Maybe she's going to live in the basement.

Billy was quiet as he walked. Thoughts tumbled, one upon the next. The black-footed ferrets, the only ones in all the world, all in one building, close enough to touch! Maybe he could meet Tom Thorne, who was in charge of breeding the ferrets, or Tom Campbell, who studied them. Tom Campbell had worked with Tim Clark. Billy had read about them all.

Billy turned down the path into the pine woods.

The path wound through the woods until it reached the pond. The water was still and black as the late-afternoon sun slanted through the trees on the far side. Billy reached the edge of the pond, where the moss was green. There he sat on his favorite rock, the large one past the open space. Billy and Zucchini spent many afternoons just quietly on that rock. Even in the snow they sat, Billy in his heaviest jacket, with sweaters underneath and a wool cap.

Billy reached back and took Zucchini out of the hood. With one hand he held Zucchini's narrow leash. The leash was attached to a tiny halter that fit securely on Zucchini's body. Billy didn't think Zucchini would run away, but he thought he might chase after a squirrel and get lost, or get hurt by another animal, and he didn't want to take the chance. He put Zucchini on his lap and stroked him gently.

"We're going to the prairie," Billy said.

The prairie! thought Zucchini. Can it be true?

"Dad wants to take us," Billy went on. "If Mom says it's O.K., we're going. We'll see other ferrets. We'll see the sagebrush and the open spaces. We'll walk together, just the two of us. I'll take off your leash so you can run. We'll see the mountains in the distance and the ones behind with snow."

Zucchini's tiny body was flooded with joy.

The prairie! he thought. My dream come true!

Drugstore Teeth

rs. Ferguson thought the trip was a wonderful idea, but Mr. Ferguson wasn't sure. Billy sat on the couch, holding Zucchini, while they discussed the situation.

"Billy should be making new friends," Mr. Ferguson was saying. "He should have a chance to get involved in the sports program."

I don't want a chance to get involved in the sports program, Billy thought. And Zucchini is my friend.

"Let them go somewhere closer," Mr. Ferguson continued. "They shouldn't take two weeks off from school. Not now."

Please let us go! thought Zucchini. I have to see the prairie!

"Why don't I ask Billy's teacher about it?" Mrs. Ferguson suggested.

Mr. Ferguson thought that was a good idea. If Billy's teacher approved of the plan, he would agree.

The next day Mrs. Ferguson met with Ms. Crystal. Ms. Crystal said she wanted to think it over. "Could I speak to you?" she asked Billy that afternoon during independent-reading time. He was reading about peregrine falcons. Billy put down his book and approached Ms. Crystal's desk. "I hear you want to go to Wyoming," she said.

"Yes," said Billy.

"You would have to keep up with your schoolwork."

"I know," said Billy.

"I have an idea," Ms. Crystal continued. She was leaning on her elbow, fingering the delicate handmade silver earring on her left ear. "Your report on black-footed ferrets was excellent."

"Thank you," said Billy.

"How would you like to expand your report? You could interview the biologists. You could keep a journal. You could include an essay on the situation from your point of view. It would be an independent-study program."

Billy's heart raced with excitement.

"Who knows?" Ms. Crystal continued. "We might submit it to one of the conservation magazines. Your experiences could interest other children in the subject. What do you think?"

"It's a good idea," said Billy. He wanted to say, "Thank you! I'd love to do the report! Thank you for letting me go!" but once again he couldn't get the words out.

The day seemed endless. Billy wanted to rush home and tell Zucchini. He wanted to buy Zucchini a traveling cage. He wanted to call his dad.

When he got off the bus, the girl who lived next door spoke to him about his report. She was the one who owned the German shepherd, Sonya. Billy knew her from class, but they had never said more than "Hello." Her name was Margaret. She had straight black hair and was very quiet, almost as quiet as Billy. Sometimes Billy would see her with her dog. Billy had liked her report. It was about a woman who raised sled dogs and won races in Alaska.

"I liked your report," Margaret said as they got off the bus.

"I liked yours, too," said Billy.

Margaret stopped at the side of the road. She hugged her books, one arm across the other. "I like dogs," she said.

"Me too," said Billy. He wanted to say something else, but he couldn't think of what.

They were quiet for several moments. Then Margaret spoke. "I like wolves, too," she said.

"So do I," said Billy.

"Good-bye," said Margaret.

"Good-bye," said Billy.

Inside the house Zucchini waited for Billy. He sat at the front of his cage, listening for the sound of the front door opening and Billy's footsteps in the hall. One-Day Service hurried on her wheel. "Find the cheese, bite the cheese, chew the cheese," she repeated as she ran.

Just then Zuchini heard the door.

He's home! he thought.

Billy dropped his books on the table in the front hall and hurried into the playroom. "We're going!" he called. "We're going to the prairie!"

Zucchini paced excitedly back and forth along the front of his cage as Billy opened the window shade. Bright sunlight flooded the room.

"We're going for three weeks!" said Billy. "My teacher said it's O.K.!"

Billy moved to Zucchini's cage. He opened the door, reached in, picked up Zucchini, and held him close. Zucchini rubbed the side of his head on Billy's shirt, nose first, several times in gratitude.

"Sonya has drugstore teeth," said Emma. She came into

the playroom wearing her kangaroo suit and eating a large piece of melon. Juice flowed down to her chin.

"What's that supposed to mean?" asked Billy.

"She doesn't have regular teeth like a puppy would have, but only gigantic Dracula teeth with those pointy vampire side ones like a wolf."

I don't like the sound of that! thought Zucchini.

Emma spit a melon seed into her kangaroo pouch. "Margaret bought them at the drugstore and stuck them in," she added.

"They're real," said Billy.

"No way," said Emma.

"She's not full-grown, but she has her permanent teeth," Billy explained. "It happens to all dogs. For a while their teeth look big."

"They're drugstore teeth," said Emma. "Margaret must have got them for Halloween, and then she didn't use them, or she used them, but then she forgot about them 'cause she put them in a jar, or a drawer, or some kind of box that she didn't remember."

"There is no such thing as drugstore teeth," said Billy.

"Think again," said Emma. The juice from the melon flowed down the front of her kangaroo suit and down her arms to her elbows. She spit another seed into her kangaroo pouch.

"Don't do that," said Billy. "They'll rot in there and smell."

"The baby eats them," said Emma.

"There's no baby," said Billy, "and there's no such thing as drugstore teeth."

"You can be wrong," said Emma. "You might be big, but you can be very wrong."

Billy let the conversation drop. Emma could be stubborn. Anyway, he wanted to tell her about the trip. "Dad's taking us to Wyoming," he said. He stood by the window, holding Zucchini, stroking him gently as he spoke. "We're taking two weeks off and adding it to our spring vacation, so it can be a long trip. We'll have three whole weeks with Dad!"

Emma stopped eating the melon. She looked at Billy, then bent her head down and spit three seeds into her pouch. "Baby kangaroos like seeds," she said. "That's why I spit them in."

Buck E. Benson

"re you excited about the trip?" Mr. Ferguson asked at dinnertime.

"What trip?" said Emma. Since she was mad at her father, she hadn't admitted they were going.

"The trip with Daddy," Mrs. Ferguson explained.

"Daddy's not going on a trip."

"Not me," said Mr. Ferguson, "your other daddy."

"One daddy is enough," said Emma.

"You have two daddies," said Mrs. Ferguson. "You're a lucky girl."

"Try it," said Emma.

"You'll have a wonderful time," said her mother. "You'll see horses and cowgirls and mountains with snow."

"Monica had a bad thing happen," said Emma, pouring extra Spiedies marinade sauce on her chicken leg. "She was running with her bike and holding it and there was this bumpy part in the road and she fell on her tonsils."

Mrs. Ferguson finished the last of her rice. "You'll have a long drive," she said. "You'll have to be patient."

"Wait a minute!" said Emma. She seemed excited. "Are we going to different states?"

"Yes," said Billy.

"Buck E. Benson's Burger Room Playshow!"

"What's that?" asked Mr. Ferguson.

"It's this restaurant that's also a fun room with games and I've been wanting to go there so much, but they only have them in certain states and mostly they don't have them."

"How do you know?" said Billy.

"Monica told me."

"Was this before she fell on her tonsils?"

"Way before and New York doesn't have them, but some other states do. Monica went on a long driving trip and she found one. You can tell 'cause Buck E.'s outside and he's this giant host that greets you."

"What is he?" asked Billy.

"He's a groundhog I think, or a hamster, I don't know, but he greets you and they have this jumping room where balls go around and they have bowling in ridged-hole places and stuffed animals and balloons."

"Is Buck E. Benson stuffed?" asked Billy.

"He's maybe stuffed with inside machine parts, or he's a person in a suit like my kangaroo suit, but more puffed out and big."

"Sounds great," said Mr. Ferguson.

"He is," said Emma. "And I'll wear my kangaroo suit every day and when Buck E. sees me he'll think I'm a kangaroo."

That evening before Billy went to bed, he and Zucchini sat on a chair by the window in Billy's room and looked out at the stars. It was a clear blue-black night. The stars shone brightly, far beyond the branches of the oak tree.

The same sky is over the prairie, thought Zucchini. I'll be there soon. And no One-Day Service! I'll be free! No noisy wheel, no endless talking. Just quiet all around and mountains and sky.

The weeks before leaving passed quickly. Billy was busy. He collected his schoolwork, got a haircut, and bought a new toothbrush, three rolls of film, a small notebook that would fit in a back pocket of his jeans, a ballpoint pen with a clip, a new pair of sneakers, and a traveling cage for Zucchini. After that he packed his blue duffel bag and he was ready.

Rubber Chicken

On the morning they were to leave, Zucchini sat in the window of the playroom and watched the sun come up. As usual, One-Day Service was running on her wheel, her mouse paws treading the metal bars with lightning speed.

I should say good-bye, Zucchini thought as he watched her run. It's only right.

The mouse hurried on, ears pressed flat to her head, eyes staring.

"I'm leaving," said Zucchini.

"No time," said the mouse.

"I'm going to the prairie," said Zucchini. "I've wanted to go there for as long as I can remember, and now's my chance."

"Have a good time," said the mouse.

Zucchini was stunned. It was the first nice thing she had said to him. "Thank you," he said.

Squeak, squeak, rattle, rattle, bang, bang, went the wheel. Zucchini watched as the mouse continued her feverish run. Now that he was leaving, he suddenly felt sorry for her. She was all alone, trapped in her cage, unable to enjoy life, unable to travel. "Would you like to go somewhere?" he asked.

"Not really," said the mouse.

"Would you like me to bring you something?"

"Like what?"

"I don't know. Some prairie grass, a desert plant, a stone?"

"Do they have any cheese?"

"I don't think so," said Zucchini. "At least I never heard of it."

"You never heard of cheese?" The mouse seemed shocked. She stared at Zucchini, ears still flat, not missing a step.

"On the prairie, I mean," said Zucchini. "I never heard of cheese on the prairie. I've heard of it in a general way. You talk about it all the time."

"Oh," said the mouse.

"Then you don't want anything?"

"Not unless you see some cheese."

"Suit yourself," said Zucchini.

"You too," said the mouse.

After breakfast Billy and Zucchini sat looking out the front window, watching for Billy's father to arrive. Billy's father had told him he had rented a Pathfinder. It had four-wheel drive, his father had explained. That meant extra safety in the snow. They were likely to run into snow, especially in the Tetons.

"See how shiny my purse is?" Emma asked. She had come into the hall, wearing her kangaroo suit and carrying a small red patent-leather purse.

"I'm busy," said Billy.

"This purse is gonna shine in the dark I bet," said Emma. She moved closer to Billy at the window. "Want to see what I have?"

"Not now," said Billy. "I'm looking for Dad."

Emma opened her purse. "I have these things," she said.

"I said I didn't want to see them."

"I have a small brush, tiny white gloves of lace, and my rubber chicken."

"You're not really going to wear that kangaroo suit to Wyoming, are you?" Billy asked.

"You bet," said Emma, "and when I see Buck E. Benson, I'll be ready."

"Ready for what?"

"Search your mind to know."

A green-and-tan Pathfinder stopped in front of the house.

"He's here!" said Billy.

That's it! thought Zucchini. We're on our way!

Billy held Zucchini tight and ran to greet his dad, who stood in the driveway holding his black steel-rimmed sunglasses. He wore his usual outfit—jeans, sneakers, a leather jacket, and a baseball cap.

Billy set Zucchini down on the grass; then he and his dad hugged a long hug. He had missed his dad so much. He felt like he was going to cry.

"You look great," his father said. He had his hands on Billy's shoulders and had backed up a step to look at his son. "You got big."

Billy felt embarrassed when his father said that, but he liked it.

"Hello, Zucchini," said Billy's father. He reached out his index finger, letting Zucchini sniff it with his eager nose. He patted Zucchini gently. "What a great guy you are."

You look nice too, thought Zucchini.

And then it happened. Mr. and Mrs. Ferguson came out of the house carrying the luggage, and behind them was Emma. She still wore her kangaroo suit. The shiny red purse hung from her left shoulder. Both arms were wrapped around the orange-plastic case. Inside was One-Day Service.

On the Road

"**I**'m ready," said Emma as she approached the car.

Oh, no, thought Zucchini.

"One-Day Service is staying here," said Mrs. Ferguson.

"No she's not," said Emma. "She's a driving mouse."

Zucchini looked up at Billy with pleading eyes.

Don't let her come! he thought.

"You can't bring her," said Billy. He could sense Zucchini's concern.

Emma stopped at the car. She took one hand off the mouse's cage and reached out for the door.

"Don't I get a hug?" asked Mr. Reynolds. That was their father's last name. It was their last name too.

Emma held up the cage. "This is my mouse," she said.

"Nice mouse," said her father.

"Her name is One-Day Service."

"Hello, One-Day Service," said Mr. Reynolds. He bent over and peered through the orange plastic at the shivering mouse. "She looks scared, or something."

"She is," said Emma.

"She's not coming," said Billy.

Emma's lower lip began to tremble, the way it did when she was about to cry. "Zucchini's coming," she said, "so why can't my mouse?"

"It's different," said Billy. "Dad and I arranged it."

Mr. Reynolds knelt down in front of Emma. "You can bring One-Day Service," he said. "It's O.K."

Oh, no, thought Zucchini.

"Maybe it's not a good idea," said Mrs. Ferguson.

"It's not!" said Billy.

"How come?" asked Mr. Reynolds.

"It's too complicated," said Mrs. Ferguson. "You're bringing one animal already."

"It's fine," said Mr. Reynolds. He turned to Emma. "Put her in the car."

Emma turned to Mr. Ferguson. He was loading Billy's duffel bag into the rear storage compartment. "I can't open the door," she said.

"I'll do it," said Mr. Reynolds.

"I want Daddy to do it," said Emma. She was looking at her stepfather.

"He's your daddy too, sweetheart," said Mr. Ferguson. "He's right by the door."

"So what?" said Emma.

Mr. Reynolds opened the door. "So there you go," he said.

Billy didn't like it when his father and stepfather were together. Things seemed tense. And Emma always made it worse.

Zucchini's heart sank as Emma reached into the back of the Pathfinder and slid the mouse's cage onto the seat.

"Now where's my hug?" asked Mr. Reynolds.

Emma paid no attention to her father. She climbed up into the car and shut the door.

"She's still mad at you for leaving," said Mrs. Ferguson.

"Looks that way," said Mr. Reynolds.

Mr. Ferguson finished loading the car, shut the rear hatch door, and came around to join the others. After they hugged good-bye, Billy bent down and picked up Zucchini. They were on their way.

Heading west toward Route 17 Zucchini felt numb. He couldn't believe what had happened. He had planned it for weeks. Freedom at last! No chatter, no wheel, no endless noise. Now One-Day Service was coming! How could he stand it? He curled up on Billy's lap and tried to sleep.

"You're quiet back there," Mr. Reynolds said to Emma. They were pulling past a large truck. SHOES FOR LESS it said in large red letters across the side. "Everything O.K.?"

"If you think so," said Emma.

"I think so," said Mr. Reynolds. "How's your mouse?"

"Hunched," said Emma.

"She's nervous," said Billy. "She doesn't like the car."

"Neither do I," said Emma.

"Why not?" asked Mr. Reynolds.

"It's a stupid trip."

On the outskirts of Binghamton they found a Pizza Pit. Billy took off Zucchini's leash and halter and put him into his traveling cage. Billy had set up a surprise. He had cut off the arm of an old sweatshirt and had placed it in the cage.

Nice sleeve, thought Zucchini.

He crawled inside the soft cotton tunnel and fell asleep.

Pizza Pit

he Pizza Pit was crowded. Just inside the door was a group of people gathered behind a black sign with white letters. THE HOSTESS WILL SEAT YO, said the sign. The U had disappeared.

"What time is it when the elephant sits on the fence?" Emma asked the teenage girl ahead of her in line.

"I don't know," said the girl. She wore a pink sweatshirt, had three small earrings in each ear, and appeared in need of sleep.

"Time to get a new elephant," said Emma.

"Really," said the girl. It was hard to tell what she meant by that.

The boy next to her was climbing on the metal stand of the THE HOSTESS WILL SEAT YO sign. He stared at Billy. Billy looked down at the floor.

"What happened to your tooth?" asked the boy. His jacket was too large for him, his shoes untied.

"I fell," said Billy.

"What did you fall on?"

"Stone steps," said Billy.

"My steps are wood," said the boy. He went back to climbing.

"I'll be right with you," said the hostess as she gathered a stack of menus. She was thin, with red hair stiff with spray and held up with a plastic clip. "How many in your party?" she asked.

"Three," said Mr. Reynolds.

"Two," said Emma. "Two people, one kangaroo."

"Right this way," said the hostess, without bothering to listen. They followed her down the three steps into the pit area and over to a table by the windows. "Here you go," she said with forced cheerfulness. She looked down at Emma. "Well, hi there. Could you be a bear?"

"See my pouch and think again."

The hostess didn't have time for that. "Well, well," she said. "Laurie will be by to serve you."

"I'm a kangaroo," said Emma.

The hostess set down the menus. "Cutest thing you ever did see," she said.

The pizza was delicious. Billy was happy, sitting next to his dad, eating his favorite food and starting the trip he had looked forward to for so long.

A short man wearing a red-and-white shirt that said GET IT AT THE PIT passed the table. He carried a tray piled high with paper plates, plastic glasses, half-finished drinks, and half-eaten pizza. He dumped the contents of the tray into a nearby garbage can.

He should recycle the plastic, Billy thought. Maybe he doesn't know. Maybe I should tell him.

I'm useless, he thought. How can I help the earth if I can't even tell people what I think?

Emma took a sip of her drink through the red-and-white-striped straw brought by Laurie. She stopped suddenly, squeezed her mouth tight, and shut her eyes. In a moment she went back to drinking.

"What was that?" asked Mr. Reynolds.

"Lemonade gives me the sparkles," said Emma.

"Me too," said her father. He paused a moment, just watching her drink. "I sure miss you guys," he said.

Emma stared at her pizza. "I wish Mom and Dad were here," she said.

"Dad's here," said Billy.

Emma didn't answer.

Mr. Reynolds pushed aside his plate, took two folded sheets of paper out of his jacket pocket, and spread them out on the table. "Look at this," he said. "Look what they can do. I ran two destinations through the computer. Our trip is all set up. They give you the shortest routes."

He said there were two basic ways of going, depending on what Billy wanted to do first. Billy said he would like to visit three places: Meeteetse, where the black-footed ferrets had been found; Jackson Hole, where Tom Campbell, a biologist who had worked with Tim Clark, had his research company; and Laramie, where a doctor named Tom Thorne ran the captive-breeding center. He didn't care which came first.

"Did you call the conservation people?" asked Billy's father.

"Not yet," said Billy.

"What if they're not there?"

Billy didn't answer. The thought of calling famous doctors and biologists and asking to meet with them was too much to think about.

"You should call them," said his father.

"Maybe tomorrow," said Billy.

They decided to take the northern route. They would head for Cody, which was near Meeteetse, then go through Yellowstone Park to Grand Teton National Park and into Jackson Hole. From there they would head east, ending up at the captive-breeding facility near Laramie. Billy could hardly wait.

"How many states do we go through?" asked Emma. She was unwrapping saltine crackers from their cellophane wrap, putting them into her pouch.

Mr. Reynolds consulted his papers. "Nine, counting New York," he answered.

"Don't bother with New York," said Emma. "He's not here."

"Who's not?" asked her father.

"Buck E. Benson," said Billy.

Laurie approached with the check. She was about seventeen years old, with brown curly hair and bright blue eyes, set wide in a cheerful face.

"Have you heard of Buck E. Benson around here?" asked Emma.

"I sure haven't," Laurie answered. "Does he play football?"

"He might," said Emma. "He does a lot of things."

Quality Rest Motel

illy and Emma and Mr. Reynolds were just readying to leave the Pizza Pit when Zucchini woke up. One-Day Service was running hard. *Squeak, squeak, rattle, rattle, bang, bang,* went the wheel as she sped on her way.

There she goes again, thought Zucchini.

He crawled out from inside Billy's sweatshirt sleeve and stared across the parking lot at the bright red-and-white sign. THE PIZZA PIT it said in bold letters, and below that, WINGS AFTER 8:00 P.M.

Wings of what? he thought. Where am I?

All at once he remembered. He was on his way to the prairie, and One-Day Service was coming too! There would be no peace.

"Have to hurry. No time. Lots of cheese," repeated the mouse as she ran.

"You have to stop that," said Zucchini. "It's too small in here."

"Where are we?" asked the mouse, not missing a step.

"We're on our way to the prairie," said Zucchini.

"Oh," said the mouse.

"You don't sound very happy," said Zucchini. "Don't you want to go?"

"Not really," said the mouse.

Heading west on Route 17, Zucchini sat up tall on Billy's

lap. The noise of the engine drowned out the sound of the wheel. Zucchini found the motion of the tires on the road to be restful.

This is nice, he thought.

Mr. Reynolds had bought Zucchini a piece of red licorice. Billy held the candy while Zucchini ate. Zucchini chewed with pleasure as he watched the sights speeding past. A group of Canada geese had gathered on a sloping lawn. Over a hundred geese stood motionless, each facing north, each looking into the sky as if picturing a journey to come.

Zucchini finished the licorice, then curled up on Billy's lap, his head upside down, his body folded like a pretzel. It was time for a nap.

Mr. Reynolds turned on the tape player. Gerry Mulligan played gentle jazz on his baritone sax. Billy's father loved jazz. "O.K. with you guys?" he asked.

"Sure," said Billy.

"I have children's tapes if anyone wants to hear them," said Emma.

"We don't," said Billy.

"After this one," said Mr. Reynolds. "Then it's your turn." He reached into the pocket of his leather jacket, pulled out the paper describing their route, and handed it to Billy. "There you go," he said. Billy was always the navigator when he drove with his dad. He liked the job.

Mr. Reynolds looked at Emma in the rearview mirror. "How are you doing back there?" he asked. "Are you getting a little bit used to me?"

"Not so much," said Emma.

"Let me know how it goes."

"I will," said Emma. "How many states do we see today?"

"Three if we're lucky," answered her father. "We'll be out of New York in four hours."

"You don't count New York."

"I forgot," said Mr. Reynolds. "They don't have Buffy Swenson."

"Buck E. Benson!"

"Right. They don't have Buck E. Benson. So that's four hours we don't count."

"You can count the hours."

"O.K."

"Just don't say the name."

"O.K. So that's four hours in the state we don't say the name of, one hour in Pennsylvania, and we'll spend the night in Ohio. We see two states."

"Not counting the one we don't say the name of."

"Right."

The Quality Rest Motel in Ashtabula, Ohio, allowed pets. "Pets are permitted in the rooms," explained the young woman behind the front desk. She was thin, with dark hair and glasses and a pale face. Her pink blush was strongly applied.

"Have you seen Buck E. Benson around here?" Emma asked the woman.

"Who?" The woman bent forward over the counter. "My, my," she said. "Are you a kangaroo?"

"Yup," said Emma. "Have you seen him?"

"Who's that?" the woman asked.

"Buck E. Benson," said Emma. "He's a hamster, or maybe a groundhog, who's stuffed I think, and gigantic and he has a restaurant that's a fun house and he's the host."

"Ah . . . no," said the woman. She seemed confused.

"He's not in Pennsylvania," said Emma. "We checked."

"Pinball machines," said Mr. Reynolds. He pointed to the alcove next to the coffee shop. He and Billy loved to play pinball together. Once on a movie location in Alabama they had played for two hours straight. Billy was happy to be with his dad.

Lost

The lightbulb in the lamp on the table between the beds was burned out. Zucchini sat on Billy's lap in the chair by the window, while Mr. Reynolds called the front desk. "We need a new lightbulb," Mr. Reynolds told the woman who answered.

The mouse was in her cage on the cabinet by the television set, running furiously. *Squeak, squeak, rattle, rattle, bang, bang,* went the wheel.

No one sleeps tonight, Zucchini thought.

Emma was watching TV. She sat on the edge of the bed, wearing her kangaroo suit, holding her stegosaurus, and eating potato chips from a small bag with an owl on it. Although Billy had explained they would only be staying one night, she had unpacked all her things. The top drawer of the bureau was open, socks, underwear, and T-shirts all in a jumble.

"Let's see if they've got a Chinese restaurant in town," said Mr. Reynolds when he hung up the phone. He loved food that came from different countries.

Emma popped a potato chip into her mouth and chewed loudly. She stared at the announcer, who spoke into the camera. "Have the nose you've always dreamed of," the woman was saying.

"Let's go," said Mr. Reynolds.

Emma turned off the TV.

Billy put Zucchini into his cage. He set the cage on the table by the window. Then he opened the curtains so Zucchini could look out. "We'll be back soon," he said.

That's good, Zucchini thought.

When they reached the elevators, Emma wanted to go back to the room. "I forgot Steggie," she said.

"Who?" her father asked.

"Her stegosaurus," said Billy.

"Don't worry," said Emma. "She's stuffed."

"Why do kids like stuffed animals so much?" Mr. Reynolds asked.

"If they weren't stuffed, they'd be flat," said Emma.

"That's true," said her father. He reached into the front pocket of his jeans and pulled out the key.

"I better do it," said Billy.

"I can manage," said Emma.

"You don't know where it is."

"It's the last door by the twisted hallway."

"There is no twisted hallway."

"It bends," said Emma.

"It turns," said Billy.

Mr. Reynolds handed Emma the key.

Zucchini sat in his cage and looked out the window as dusk settled over the parking lot. A large sign lit up the entrance.

WELCOME HARDWARE STORE EMPLOYEES

OF EAST TRUMBELL

said the sign.

Just then Emma opened the door. She moved to the mouse's cage. "Hello, One-Day Service," she said. "You're verrry white." She opened the orange-plastic cage, reached in, and took the shivering mouse off the wheel. "I love your toes," she said. She held the mouse for a moment, then looked down at the open clothes drawer. "I'm going to put you in this drawer," she said. She dropped the terrified mouse into the drawer on top of a tumble of colored socks.

She won't like that, thought Zucchini.

"Have a nice rest," Emma told the mouse. She moved to the bed, picked up her stegosaurus, and left, slamming the door behind her.

Zucchini looked about the room. It was brown. Brown carpet, brown curtains, brown bedspreads, brown walls. There was a picture of fruit above each of the beds and an ice bucket on the corner table. Standing paper signs announced bargains at the coffee shop and entertainment in the lounge. One-Day Service was shivering in Emma's clothes drawer.

She's really scared, Zucchini thought.

He stood up and peered through the narrow bars of his

cage. "Are you all right in there?" he asked.

The mouse didn't answer. She continued to crouch on the sock pile, her body shaking, her ears flat, her eyes wide.

"Are you all right?" Zucchini repeated, louder this time.

"Where am I?" asked the mouse.

"You're in the clothes drawer."

"It's too big."

"It's not that big," said Zucchini. "It seems big to you because you're so small."

There was a knock on the door.

What's that? thought Zucchini.

"Don't hurt me!" said the mouse.

The door opened and a man came in. He breathed heavily and carried a lightbulb. "Maintenance," he said as he switched on the ceiling light. Leaving the door open, he moved into the room.

Zucchini's heart pounded in his chest.

What does he want? he thought. Billy didn't say anything about a man coming in.

The man made a kind of sighing noise, as if life was too much for him, or his shift was too long. He looked about the room. "Which lamp?" he said to himself.

One-Day Service was shaking in the drawer. "Oh, no, oh, no, oh, no," she said. She began darting in all directions, under the socks, over the undershirts, around the pajamas. "Oh, no, oh, no, oh, no."

The man moved toward the lamp on the cabinet.

"Get away!" said the mouse.

"Maybe this one," said the man. He reached for the lamp. Then he saw Zucchini. "What's that?" he asked. Zucchini stared at him with frightened eyes. "Must be some kind of weasel," said the man. "They'll bring anything." He switched on the lamp, his large stomach bumping into the open drawer.

"Oh, no!" said One-day Service. With a flying leap she charged up the mound of colored socks and out over the top of the drawer. Landing with a tiny thud on the brown carpet, she huddled in the corner by the closet, her mind locked in terror.

"Don't kill me! Don't crush me!" she called. Then she began to run.

"Calm yourself," said Zucchini.

One-Day Service was shaking as she ran.

"Where are you going?" called Zucchini.

There was no answer. Eyes bulging, ears flat to her head, One-Day Service darted around the cabinet, into the closet, out of the closet, under the table, behind the curtains, under the beds, into the bathroom, out of the bathroom, around the luggage, out the door, and down the hall.

Mouth String

"You didn't eat much," Mr. Reynolds said to Emma as they finished the lemon chicken.

"It sours my joints," said Emma.

During dessert Billy talked about black-footed ferrets and how they were among the rarest mammals on earth. "They're endangered," he explained. "Zucchini looks like one, but he's probably not."

"He'd better not be," said his father.

"What do you mean?"

"You couldn't keep him."

"I know," said Billy.

"You sure he's not?"

"Pretty sure," said Billy. "The lady at the ASPCA gave him to me. She wouldn't do that if he was endangered."

"People do weird things." Mr. Reynolds cracked open his fortune cookie. "It's a good idea to find out before you go around breaking the law."

Billy's stomach sank like an elevator plunging down inside a skyscraper.

Don't let him be a black-footed ferret! he thought. I should have asked! How could I have been so stupid?

Zucchini paced back and forth inside his tiny cage. He felt trapped. The man had left, shutting the door, and One-Day Service was gone, running terrified somewhere in the building. Or somewhere out of the building. That would be worse!

She's lost, Zucchini thought. Frightened and lost. And I can't get out to find her!

Suddenly he stopped.

Wait a minute, he thought. Why am I upset? I can't stand her. Why do I want to bring her back?

He didn't know why, but the feeling was strong.

Someone's got to find her, he thought. She could get caught somewhere, or crushed, or stepped on. She could get out of the building and get hit by a car! I don't like her, but I don't want her to get hurt. If Billy were here, he could let me out. Maybe I could find her.

He paced back and forth inside his tiny cage, awaiting Billy's return.

Mr. Reynolds was the first to come in. "Bedtime, Emma," he said. "We're getting up early."

"Kangaroos are always early," said Emma. She barged past her father and into the bathroom.

Billy was still upset. The idea of losing Zucchini was too much to bear. He followed his father into the room. Zucchini was pacing faster now in an attempt to get Billy to notice that something was wrong. Billy would usually have understood in an instant, but he was too worried now.

Mr. Reynolds put his arm around his son. "I doubt he's a black-footed ferret," he said. "I just think you should check it out."

"What if he is?" asked Billy.

I don't care what I am, thought Zucchini. Let me out!

"He was given to you by the ASPCA," said Mr. Reynolds. "They specialize in animal welfare. They thought he should be with you."

"Maybe they made a mistake."

"Ask them."

Zucchini was pacing faster now. He began scratching at the bottom of the cage. "What's wrong?" Billy asked. He moved to the cage, opened the door, and took Zucchini out. The tiny ferret struggled to get free.

"What is it?" Billy asked. He set Zucchini down on the carpet. "What's wrong?"

Zucchini ran to the door and Billy followed.

Mr. Reynolds stretched out on one of the beds. He tried the lamp on the bedside table. "They fixed it," he said.

"Can I use the mouth string?" Emma called from the bathroom.

"The what?" said Mr. Reynolds.

"Dental floss," said Billy. He was kneeling by Zucchini at the door.

"O.K., but hurry," said Mr. Reynolds. He leaned up against the pillows, his eyes resting on the empty mouse's cage. "Where's your mouse?"

"I can't hear you," Emma called.

"Where's your mouse?"

Zucchini was pacing rapidly, sniffing at the crack beneath the door.

"What's wrong?" asked Billy. "Is something out there? Why are you so scared?"

Ice Machine

mma came out of the bathroom carrying her tiny toothbrush with the pig's face on the handle. "I couldn't hear you," she said. "My mouth was full."

"Where's your mouse?" her father asked.

"She's in the drawer," said Emma. "She wanted to be cozy."

She's not cozy now, thought Zucchini.

He was scratching at the crack beneath the door.

Emma began rummaging through the clothes drawer. "Where is she?" she asked.

Zucchini was scratching furiously, his sharp nails making tiny streaks on the inside of the door.

"What is it?" asked Billy. "What's wrong?"

Mr. Reynolds joined Emma at the drawer. "She must be under all this stuff," he said, peering into the jumble of clothes. "This is not a good place for her."

"She's not here!" said Emma. She began pulling clothes out of the drawer, throwing them on the floor.

"Be careful," said Mr. Reynolds. "You'll never find her that way."

"One-Day Service!" said Emma. "My mouse!"

Zucchini stopped scratching and stared up at Billy, pleading with his eyes for him to open the door.

In an instant Billy knew. "She's in the hall."

"How do you know?" asked Mr. Reynolds.

"Zucchini knows."

"My mouse!" said Emma. She ran to the door.

"Wait!" said Billy.

Emma knew when Billy was serious. She stood still as he ran to his duffel bag and pulled out Zucchini's leash and halter.

Hurry! thought Zucchini. Every second counts with a mouse.

"Maybe she's still in the drawer," said Mr. Reynolds, searching through Emma's socks.

"She's not," said Billy.

"My mouse!" cried Emma.

Billy returned to Zucchini, putting on the halter and attaching the leash. When he opened the door, Emma ran into the hall and down toward the elevators. "One-Day Service!" she called. "Where are you?"

Zucchini lifted his head high.

"Can you find her?" Billy asked.

Zucchini's nose twitched as he quickly picked up the scent of the mouse. In moments Emma ran back from the elevators. "She's nowhere!" Emma called.

"Quiet," said Billy. He held the end of the leash as Zucchini pulled ahead, zigzagging across the carpet, following the scent.

"Maybe she's outside!" cried Emma. "Maybe she's dead!"

"Quiet," said Billy.

"Look!" said Mr. Reynolds. "Zucchini has the scent!"

Emma and Mr. Reynolds watched as Zucchini led Billy down the hall past the elevators to the ice machine. It had a loud motor and stood in an alcove next to two other machines, one for drinks and one for snacks. Zucchini stuck his nose beneath the noisy ice maker.

She's under here, he thought. I can smell her.

Billy took off Zucchini's halter. "Be careful," he said.

The opening beneath the ice machine was narrow. Zucchini stuck his nose into the dark space. Stretching himself to his longest and thinnest shape, he began pulling himself forward.

Don't let him get stuck in there, thought Billy. Please!

Zucchini inched his way forward in the dark. All at once he stopped.

What am I doing? he thought. Rescuing a mouse I can't stand so she can torment me for the rest of my life? I must be crazy!

He could hear the sound of One-Day Service squeaking in fear.

"I'm coming," he said.

It was too dark to see, but Zucchini could sense the body heat of the mouse. He could feel her fear. All at once his nose touched her body. He turned his head to the side, gently gripping her tail between his teeth. Then he began to back up, easing himself along the floor through the narrow space beneath the groaning machine.

I can't believe I'm doing this, he thought. Most ferrets would have eaten this mouse by now.

Slowly he moved back, inch by inch, dragging the terrified mouse. Pretty soon Billy could see Zucchini's tail, and then his rear quarters, backing out from under the ice maker.

"Does he have my mouse?" asked Emma. She was on her hands and knees, her forehead pressed against the bottom of the machine.

Just then all of Zucchini appeared. There was One-Day Service, dirty and shivering, her hairless mouse tail trapped between Zucchini's teeth.

Letter

Emma wanted to give One-Day Service a bath. Mr. Reynolds said it wasn't a good time for washing mice, and Emma got upset. She said she didn't want to wash mice, she wanted to wash one mouse who belonged to her and was dirty. When her father still said no, she cried and said she wanted to go back to her real daddy and that Mr. Reynolds had a head like a kidney bean. Mr. Reynolds held her and said he was sorry she missed her other daddy, but that he loved her and that they would have fun on their trip. He let her wear her kangaroo suit to bed.

Zucchini watched from his cage by the window. He was exhausted from the excitement of the night. One-Day Service had thanked him several times on the way back from the ice machine. "I was happy to do it," Zucchini told her, but later when the mouse started up on her wheel, Zucchini had second thoughts.

What did I do? he thought. I should have let her go. She probably would have been fine.

Billy pulled the covers up over his head. He was trying to drown out the sound of wheel, but more than that he was trying to block out his fear.

If Zucchini is a black-footed ferret and I keep him, I'll be breaking the law, Billy thought. I can't do that. I'll have to show him to the biologists. What if they take him away?

Squeak, squeak, rattle, rattle, bang, bang.

Mr. Reynolds couldn't sleep either and finally removed the wheel from the cage.

The next morning Billy decided to write Miss Pickett a letter. He sat on the floor of the bathroom, Zucchini at his side, organizing his thoughts on a sheet of paper he had taken from his notebook.

Zucchini could sense Billy's worry. He licked Billy's arm from his wrist to his elbow, washing it with his rough tongue. He liked to show his love this way. He also liked the salty taste of Billy's skin. Crawling into Billy's lap, he turned his head upside down and nudged Billy's arm with his nose.

With his left hand Billy scratched Zucchini's triangle-shaped chin. He started to write, but after two words he stopped.

Miss Pickett won't remember me, he thought. She's busy. She doesn't have time to write to kids, especially kids she doesn't remember.

He looked down at Zucchini.

I have to write! he thought. I have to know if I can keep you!

This is what he wrote:

Dear Miss Pickett,

My name is Billy. When I was at the ASPCA you gave me Zucchini. One day you said he was a black-footed ferret. I was wondering something. How can I keep him if he's endangered? Please answer quickly.

Billy

Billy wrote the letter neatly on a fresh sheet of paper. Then he put his address at the bottom. He decided to call his mother and ask her to watch for Miss Pickett's answer in the mail. He would call his mother before meeting the biologists to see if the answer had come. If Miss Pickett said Zucchini was not a black-footed ferret, that would solve everything. She was an expert. She would know. If she said he was a black-footed ferret, or if he didn't get an answer at all, he would have to figure out what to do. He would have to get an envelope from the lady at the front desk. He didn't want to ask her, but he had no choice.

I have to send this, he told himself. I want to help animals and save the earth. At least I can ask for an envelope!

Mr. Dunderbaks

They reached the outskirts of Toledo in time for lunch. Zucchini and One-Day Service stayed in their cages on the backseat of the Pathfinder while the others went into the restaurant to eat.

Zucchini looked up at the sign above the door.

MR. DUNDERBAKS RESTAURANT SAUSAGE

What is restaurant sausage? Zucchini wondered. I thought sausage was sausage no matter where you found it. Maybe Billy will bring me some. It sounds good, whatever it is.

One-Day Service was on her wheel. She was still dusty from her time under the ice machine. Zucchini curled up on his sweatshirt sleeve and watched her run. He remembered the night before.

I should have left her alone, he thought. She wanted to go somewhere. She probably would have been fine.

Squeak, squeak, rattle, rattle, bang, bang, went the wheel.

I could have had quiet at last, Zucchini thought. Now it's too late.

Billy and Mr. Reynolds were looking at their menus.

"I'm having french fries," said Emma. Steggie was on the table next to her water glass.

Two elderly ladies approached the table. One stopped behind Emma's chair. She was short, and bent over toward Emma, whispering in her ear. "Are you a kangaroo?" she asked.

"Yup," said Emma.

"My, my," said the woman. She looked at Steggie. "Isn't he a nice dinosaur?"

"He's a girl," said Emma.

"A girl dinosaur," said the woman. "My, my."

"Don't be surprised," said Emma. "Everything has girls."

"Yes, indeed," said the woman. "Aren't you a smart one. And is your dinosaur having lunch?"

"She can't open her mouth," said Emma.

The women moved off to find their table.

That afternoon Emma took a nap in the car. Before going

to sleep, she made Billy promise on everything he cared about in this lifetime to wake her if he saw Buck E. Benson. Billy said he would.

Zucchini curled up on Billy's lap.

Soon we'll be on the prairie! he thought. Then I'll be free! No cage, no mouse, no wheel! Just the wind and the air and the sunshine and the prairie stretching out in all directions.

Billy was doing his homework. He was trying not to worry about losing Zucchini, but it was hard. He rested his notebook gently on top of Zucchini and tried to concentrate.

"When are you going to call the conservation people?" Mr. Reynolds asked. He wore his baseball hat and sunglasses and was eating a candy bar.

"I don't know," said Billy.

"You better call them soon." Billy's father often pushed Billy to get past his shyness. He didn't like to see Billy afraid of things. He knew that didn't make Billy happy.

Billy looked down at the math problem he was doing. He didn't say anything.

"Are you going to call them?" his father asked.

"Maybe," said Billy. Now he had another reason for not wanting to call. It wasn't just his shyness. Once the doctors and biologists saw Zucchini, they might say Billy couldn't keep him.

"You'd better call," said Mr. Reynolds. "We don't want to miss them."

Billy wasn't so sure.

At the Rockford Motor Inn, in Rockford, Illinois, Emma discovered her first loose tooth.

"Congratulations," said Mr. Reynolds. He had his finger

on the tooth, testing it for looseness.

"It gives me the beejies," said Emma.

"Don't worry about it," said Mr. Reynolds. "It'll fall out soon."

"Will it hurt?"

"No," said Mr. Reynolds.

"How do you know?"

"Ask Billy."

"He's not here."

Billy was out walking Zucchini in a grassy area at the side of the motel.

"Ask him when he comes back," said Mr. Reynolds.

"When will he come back?"

"Soon," said Mr. Reynolds. "Don't worry. I'll watch out for you."

"You don't help my beejies."

"What are beejies?" Mr. Reynolds stretched out on one of the narrow beds.

"Creeps," said Emma. "You know, those heejie-beejies."

"Oh yes," her father said. "I get those sometimes."

"You do?" Emma sat down on the edge of the bed. For the first time since they had left, she looked directly into her father's eyes. "They're scary, aren't they?"

"They are."

"I don't like them."

"Neither do I."

"When do you get the beejies?" Emma asked.

"Different times," her father answered.

"Like when?"

"Like when I have to go into a dark basement, or before

a storm when it's quiet and there's no wind."

"Me too," said Emma. "When else?"

"When I'm nervous about something and I don't know what it is."

"The same with me. Do you call it the heejie-beejies?"

"I call it the heebie-jeebies, but it's the same thing."

"I know," said Emma. She stretched out on the bed next to her father, and they lay quiet for a while.

Twenty Questions

The next two days were a blur of life on the road. Zucchini found a wonderful place to rest. He stretched out on top of Billy's shoulders like a collar around Billy's neck. His rear legs hung down by Billy's left ear. His nose pointed toward the window. The back of the seat wedged him snugly between its leather firmness and the warmth of Billy's neck. The noise of the engine blocked out the noise of One-Day Service's wheel, as well as her endless chatter. Although Zucchini welcomed the quiet, it seemed sad to him that the mouse talked on while no one listened.

Emma kept looking for Buck E. Benson. Still wearing her kangaroo suit (she had taken it off only once, when she took a bath in Rockford), she sat next to her mouse's cage in the backseat, Steggie on her lap, her forehead pressed against the window. "He must be somewhere," she would say every once in a while, but Buck E. was not to be seen.

Gerry Mulligan played on the tape deck as they left Illinois and crossed through southern Wisconsin. The road was straight and flat.

Mr. Reynolds enjoyed driving. He kept his eyes on the road while Billy did his homework, or they talked or played Twenty Questions with Emma. "I have one," Emma would announce, looking for Buck E. Benson as she spoke. "It's part of an animal."

"That's too much of a clue," Billy would say. "Just say animal."

"Animal."

"Is it in this car?"

"Yes."

"Is it small?"

"Yes."

"Is it in the front seat?"

"No."

"Is it in the backseat?"

"It's on something that's in something that's on the back-seat."

"That's too much of a clue."

Finally, Billy or Mr. Reynolds would say, "Is it one of One-Day Service's toenails?" and Emma would say, "Which one?" At last they would guess it.

Emma enjoyed other games, like Count the Red Cars, a game she made up, and I Packed My Grandmother's Bag, but Twenty Questions was her favorite. She also did a lot of singing. She especially liked long songs like "100 Bottles of Beer on the Wall" or songs like "Around the Corner and Under the Tree" that didn't have an end.

At one point, after entering Minnesota, they passed a factory. Billy watched the dark smoke rising into the air.

Someday I'll do something to help clean up the environment, he thought. I have to figure it out.

"Look at that," Mr. Reynolds complained. "There's pollution everywhere."

"Is garbage pollution?" asked Emma. She was eating popcorn from a cardboard tub.

"Sometimes," said Billy.

"I know how to stop it," said Emma. "I thought of it in my mind."

"How's that?" asked Mr. Reynolds.

"Pigs."

"What about them?" asked Billy.

"Well, if everybody in the world had a pig, let's say it could be a potbellied pig because they get fat and hungry, then all the pigs could eat the garbage and if maybe someone didn't have any money so they couldn't buy a pig, there could be a pig place where everybody who didn't have a pig could go and bring their garbage and there would be hungry pigs all in a circle who would eat it."

"Why would they be in a circle?" asked Billy.

"It's to my way."

"It wouldn't work," said Billy. "A lot of garbage is poison, like nuclear waste, and pigs couldn't eat that."

"Well, for that there's a special ray that could destroy it, but the science people didn't think of it yet. You shoot the bad garbage with this special zapping gun that would be like a laser, but it wouldn't cut. It would only smash up the particles and suck them into nothingness."

"Sounds good," said Mr. Reynolds.

"It is," said Emma, "but your average person could just get a pig."

Prairie

hey left the Quiet Night Motel in Blue Earth, Minnesota, at dawn. Mr. Reynolds said he wanted to push it.

"Push what?" Emma asked. She sat on the edge of her cot half-awake, her furry kangaroo legs dangling off the side.

"The trip," said Mr. Reynolds. He was pacing back and forth across the room in his undershorts, brushing his teeth. He always brushed his teeth that way. Billy figured he must get restless standing at the sink. "We have to make time today," Mr. Reynolds continued. "I want to get to Rapid City by tonight."

"Rapid City, South Dakota?" said Billy, pulling his T-shirt over his head.

"Right," said Mr. Reynolds. "We have to cross the state."

Billy's heart raced with excitement. Crossing the state meant the West! Western South Dakota! That's where Tim

Clark had spotted his first black-footed ferret. He pulled on his jeans and fastened his belt. "Can we stop at the prairie?" he asked.

"Sure," his father answered.

Zucchini was curled up inside his sweatshirt sleeve when he heard the word *prairie*. He pulled himself out of the sleeve and stood, peering at Billy through the narrow bars of his cage. He began pacing back and forth as Billy opened the cage, reached in, and picked him up. "We'll see the prairie today," Billy said.

Today? thought Zucchini. Let's go!

The trip through South Dakota seemed endless. Mr. Reynolds was getting tired of driving, Emma was getting tired of not finding Buck E. Benson, and Billy and Zucchini were impatient to get to the prairie.

In the afternoon they moved into the western part of the state. The land was changing now. There were fewer stores and signs, fewer farms and fences. Billy's heart beat loudly. Zucchini could feel that Billy was as excited as he was.

"We're here!" said Billy.

Mr. Reynolds stopped the car at the side of the road. "There's your prairie," he said.

Zucchini stared in wonder.

How beautiful! he thought.

There was not a house to be seen, not a sign, not a mall. No trees, no hills, just open country for as far as the eye could see.

"It's too big," said Emma.

"You're crazy," said Billy.

"It's not cozy, 'cause it doesn't have sides."

Billy turned to his father. "Can I take Zucchini out?" he asked.

Yes! thought Zucchini.

"Go ahead," said Mr. Reynolds.

Zucchini's heart was racing. He jumped down onto Billy's lap as Billy opened the door.

"I'm staying in the car," said Emma.

"I'll stay with you," said Mr. Reynolds.

Billy stepped down from the high seat of the Pathfinder. Holding Zucchini close, he turned to shut the door. Then he set Zucchini down. With Zucchini's leash in one hand, he faced the sun. Together they walked away from the car and out onto the prairie. Zucchini felt the earth beneath his paws, its dry pebbly firmness, its gentle grass. The air was fresh and clear.

I'm really here! he thought as he walked, a tiny spot in the vastness of space. It's more beautiful than I ever imagined.

The afternoon sun was low. All was bathed in a gold-and-rose-colored light. They crossed the prairie earth and tender grass, the sage in gentle clumps. On they walked, breathing deeply, listening to the stillness.

After some time Billy stopped. He bent down to Zucchini. "I'll let you off the leash," he said, "but you have to come back."

Zucchini looked across the open land.

I never want to leave this place, he thought.

Billy unsnapped Zucchini's leash. "Run," he said.

Zucchini ran. He ran as he had never run before. He ran free, a part of all the world, of all the sky, of everything that ever was or ever would be. Billy stood and watched his pet, and when he called him back, Zucchini came.

Cody

On the northeastern edge of the Bighorn Mountains, they picked up Route 14. They were in Wyoming now. Zucchini sat tall on Billy's lap, his front paws on the ledge of the window. The mountains rose high into the bright-blue sky. There was not a cloud to be seen. The pines were tall. Zucchini could smell their rich pine odor through the opening at the top of the window. It made him think of Oppermans Pond. The smell was just the same.

Soon they would be in Cody, where they would be spending the night. Billy could hardly believe it. Tomorrow they would see Meeteetse, the place where the black-footed ferrets had been found. Billy knew the story well. A dog named Shep found a ferret by his food bowl. His owner called the authorities, and soon the biologists came to look for more. Tim Clark did his research in Meeteetse. Dr. Thorne worked there and Tom Campbell and all the rest. From that very land they gathered the last six black-footed ferrets in all the world and took them into captivity to try and save the species.

They arrived in Cody just before nightfall. The first thing Billy did was to call his mother to see if she had heard from Miss Pickett. Mrs. Ferguson was happy to hear from Billy. She said she missed him, but had heard nothing from the ASPCA. Billy's questions remained unanswered.

Zucchini stayed in the room with One-Day Service while

Billy and Emma and Mr. Reynolds went out. He sat in his cage on the windowsill of the room at the Holiday Inn and stared out at yet another parking lot, at yet another sign. This one said:

THE MAGIC FINGERS OF
LUTHER CUTHBURT IN THE LOUNGE

One-Day Service was busy on her wheel. *Squeak, squeak, rattle, rattle, bang, bang.*

I can't stand it, thought Zucchini. Now that I've been on the prairie, it's worse. It's so beautiful out there and quiet, so noisy in here and cramped. I wish I could stay on the prairie forever! But if I stay on the prairie, I have to leave Billy. I could never do that!

Billy and Emma and Mr. Reynolds walked together down the wide street in the center of town, looking into the cafés and restaurants and shops. Emma wore her kangaroo suit and carried her shiny red purse. "It's very loose," she said as they walked.

"What is?" her father asked. He was looking at some cowboy boots in a store window.

"My tooth," said Emma. "I'm pushing it with my tongue, so I know."

"Nice boots," said Mr. Reynolds.

"There's one problem," said Emma.

"What's that?"

"Does the Tooth Fairy know the way to the Holiday Inn?"

"Absolutely. I have to go in here for a minute." Mr. Reynolds had been wanting a certain kind of waterproof windbreaker jacket and had spotted one in the window of a camping store. Billy and Emma followed him inside.

The store was big with high ceilings and brick walls and old-fashioned wooden counters. Mr. Reynolds bought the jacket. He picked one out for Billy in a smaller size and bought Emma a pair of hiking boots.

"What time is it when the elephant sits on the fence?" Emma asked the young woman in the flowered blouse behind the register.

"I don't know," said the woman. She was folding the jackets with a pleasant attention to detail.

"Time to get a new elephant," said Emma.

"That's funny," said the woman.

"It's a joke," said Emma. "How come you didn't mention I'm a kangaroo?"

"Give her time," said Mr. Reynolds.

"I thought that's what you were," said the woman. "Are you in town for a visit?"

"That's right," said Emma.

"We're on a family adventure," Mr. Reynolds explained. He told Billy to tell the woman where they were going, but Billy didn't want to. He didn't think the woman would care.

"Tell her," his father insisted.

"I'm studying ferrets," said Billy.

"I guess you're seeing Jack Turnell at Pitchfork," said the woman.

"Maybe," said Billy. He had read about Jack Turnell. He was the manager of the Pitchfork Ranch, where the ferrets had been found.

"He's real nice," said the woman. "Have a good time over there."

"Thank you," said Billy.

At dinner Mr. Reynolds suggested that Billy call Mr. Turnell and see if he could get an interview.

I can't, thought Billy. I don't know him. He won't want to talk to me.

"We came all the way out here to meet these people," Mr. Reynolds continued. "You should give it a try."

He's right, Billy thought. I want to help the animals. I want to help the earth. I have to ask questions, or I'll never learn how.

Before dinner arrived, Billy went to the phone outside the kitchen. His heart pounded as he called information, got the number, and made his call. No one answered.

Meeteetse

illy tried his call again in the morning. This time a man answered. "Hello," said the man.

Billy's heart skipped a beat. "Jack Turnell please," said Billy.

"This is he."

Billy's throat felt like it was closing up. "My name is Billy Reynolds," he said as best he could. "I live in New York and I'm studying ferrets for school."

"Good for you," said Mr. Turnell.

Billy cleared his throat. "Some magazines said they found ferrets on your ranch, so I wanted to see it."

"You came a long way," said Mr. Turnell.

"I know," said Billy.

"Come on by," said Mr. Turnell.

"O.K.," said Billy. "Thank you."

He was so excited, he could hardly write down the directions.

They picked up Route 290 at Meeteetse. A small river ran along its winding way on the right side of the gravel road. Zucchini watched from his perch on Billy's shoulder as they drove. Deer raced on the right among the soft trees. Ahead in the distance were the beautiful snow-capped mountains.

What a spot! thought Zucchini.

A deer jumped over some low bushes, then disappeared behind the thicker trees.

"Look!" said Billy. It was a thrill to see animals in the wild. Normally he didn't have the chance. He took out his notebook and his ballpoint pen with the clip and began taking notes for his report. "Pitchfork Ranch, Meeteetse," he wrote. "River. Mountains. Deer."

Soon they saw signs for the Pitchfork Ranch. The prairie opened up suddenly on the right. Antelope raced across the prairie grass. Mr. Reynolds stopped the car so Billy could take a picture.

Let's get out! thought Zucchini. This is the most beautiful place in the world!

They pulled up in front of the wooden ranch office, and Billy opened the car door.

Here we go! thought Zucchini.

Billy lifted Zucchini off his shoulder, stepped down, and carried him around to the back of the Pathfinder. He opened the hatch and put him into his cage. "You have to stay here," Billy said.

Why? thought Zucchini. We're at the prairie. I have to come with you! You promised!

Billy shut Zucchini's cage. He wanted to take him, but he couldn't. He was afraid to show him to Mr. Turnell until he had heard from Miss Pickett.

I have to be sure he isn't a black-footed ferret, Billy thought. If he is, and Mr. Turnell sees him, I'll have to give him up.

Billy wanted to explain this to Zucchini, but he didn't want to worry him. All he could say was "You have to stay here."

Why can't I come? Zucchini thought.

Billy shut the hatch.

Mr. Turnell greeted them warmly as he came out of his office. He wore a red vest and a black cowboy hat.

"Thanks for inviting us over," said Mr. Reynolds as they climbed the two wooden steps to the porch.

"Happy to do it," said Mr. Turnell. He shook hands with Mr. Reynolds.

"My tooth is loose," said Emma.

"Well now," said Mr. Turnell.

"Did you ever see a kangaroo with a loose tooth?" asked Emma.

"Can't say that I have," said Mr. Turnell.

"You can now," said Emma.

They followed Mr. Turnell into the office. A map of Wyoming hung on the wall behind a large desk. "Have a seat," said Mr. Turnell. He motioned to the leather couch by the window, where they sat. Mr. Turnell sat behind his desk. There was a moment of quiet.

I have to say something, thought Billy, but nothing came out.

"So you want to know about ferrets," said Mr. Turnell.

"Yes," said Billy.

"He has one," said Emma.

Billy's heart skipped a beat.

"What kind of ferret do you have?" asked Mr. Turnell.

"Domestic, I guess," said Billy.

"Where did you get him?"

"New York," said Billy. His heart was beating fast.

"He's in the car," said Emma.

Oh, no! thought Billy. Why did she say that?

"You brought him along?" asked Mr. Turnell.

"Yes," said Billy.

Mr. Turnell shifted in his chair. "So," he said. "What can I do for you?"

Thank God! Billy thought. He didn't ask to see him!

He was filled with a sense of relief, then quickly realized he should say something. He stared at his sneakers, but no thoughts came.

Luckily, Mr. Turnell continued. "There's a lot of points of view on ferrets," he said. "Everybody's got their opinions— the ranchers, the conservation people, the oil people, the government—but I'll tell you, we can all work together."

"I know," said Billy.

"Would you like to see where they found the ferrets?"

"Sure," said Billy.

Out in the car Zucchini was worried. He sat in his travel-ing cage, peering through the bars and out the rear window of the Pathfinder. The prairie stretched ahead for miles, all the way to the snow-capped mountains on the horizon. One-Day Service was treading her wheel. Nose high, eyes fixed on her water bottle, she ran. She seemed not to notice where they were, parked on the edge of paradise.

Squeak, squeak, rattle, rattle, bang, bang.

I have to get out of here, thought Zucchini. I have to get to the prairie!

Just then Billy, Mr. Reynolds, Mr. Turnell, and Emma came out the door of the office.

Here they come! Zucchini thought. Now he'll take me!

Billy came down the stairs with the others. They climbed into Mr. Turnell's dark-blue truck and pulled off.

Oh, no! thought Zucchini. They're going to the prairie without me. Something's wrong!

Lucille's Café

"What kind of fencing is that?" asked Mr. Reynolds as they drove down the dirt road. A row of wooden crisscross fencing bordered the road on each side.

"Buck 'n' pole," said Mr. Turnell from under his cowboy hat.

Billy was thinking of Zucchini.

I shouldn't have left him, he thought. I should have explained.

The road ended suddenly. Mr. Turnell continued driving and they found themselves on the prairie. An enormous herd of antelope raced in the distance. "That's where they found the ferrets," said Mr. Turnell, pointing up ahead. Soon he stopped the truck. They got out and Billy took a picture as they walked. Mr. Turnell showed them the large mounds of dirt with the holes in the center. "Prairie-dog holes," he said.

Billy could hear the *chip-chip*ping and the *cluck-cluck*ing sounds of the prairie dogs warning each other of the presence of humans. Mr. Turnell pointed to a small furry creature, sitting on its hind legs, high on a mound of dirt, its nose twitching with concern. "Prairie dog," he said.

Billy had read so much about this very spot, and now he was here! He wished he could show it to Zucchini, but that would have to wait.

Zucchini was upset.

Why did he leave me? he thought as he waited for Billy's return.

Squeak, squeak, rattle, rattle, bang, bang. One-Day Service was on her wheel.

"STOP!" said Zucchini in his loudest voice.

The mouse stopped. She gripped the wheel in terror with her tiny toes. She stayed that way, frozen in panic, for several moments, then got off the wheel and sat in the middle of her cage, shivering and rounded in fear. "I don't mean to bother you," she said.

"BUT YOU DO!"

There was a pause as the mouse hunched more tightly, trembling, eyes bulging wide.

"I'm sorry," said Zucchini. "I'm sorry I scared you."

"Everything scares me," said the mouse.

"Why is that?"

"I'm small."

"So am I," said Zucchini.

"You're not small to me."

"I'm small to a turkey."

"That doesn't help," said the mouse.

"Well, something has to," said Zucchini. "I can't stand the noise. Is that why you run all the time? Because you're scared? Are you trying to escape?"

"That's part of it," said the mouse.

"What's the other part?"

"I don't know," said the mouse.

"Who should I ask?"

"Me! But I have no answer. Be a little patient. Try to understand."

"I'm trying," said Zucchini.

"Try harder," said the mouse.

Billy was quiet during lunch. He sat with his father and Emma at a small table in the back of Lucille's Café on the main street of Meeteetse. The restaurant belonged to Lucille, the lady whose dog had found the ferret by his food bowl. Lucille had honored her dog's discovery by putting pictures of ferrets up everywhere. The menu said FERRET DEN across the front.

"I thought you'd like this place," said Emma as they waited for the waitress to bring their food. "It's all about ferrets, but you just sit like a grouchy thing and don't even smile."

"Mind your own business," said Billy.

Mr. Reynolds turned to his son. "What's wrong?" he asked.

Billy had a lot on his mind. He couldn't stop worrying that Zucchini might really be a black-footed ferret, that he might have to give him up. He also felt bad about going to the prairie without him. He wished he could have explained. And now there was another thing. He was upset with himself for being so shy with Mr. Turnell. He had been afraid to ask one single question.

"What's wrong?" repeated his father.

"I'm stupid," said Billy.

"Only sometimes," said Emma.

Billy ignored his sister. "I didn't ask one question," he said.

"Don't worry about it," said Mr. Reynolds.

"I have to," said Billy. "I have to learn. No one cares about the animals. I have to help."

"You will," said his father.

"How?" said Billy. "I have to talk to people. I have to ask questions and tell them my ideas."

"There's a wonderful thing called a naked mole rat," said Emma, "and it's really what I want."

"Let Billy talk," said Mr. Reynolds.

"It's completely hairless."

"Tell me later," said Mr. Reynolds.

"I want to tell you now."

"I'm talking to Billy."

"A naked mole rat would make him smile. They're amusing and wrinkled."

"Shut up for once," said Billy.

The waitress arrived with their lunch. Mr. Reynolds was hungry and began eating right away. "You'll get over it," he told Billy through a large bite of sandwich. "You need practice."

"Practice makes perfect," said Emma. "That's what Mrs. Shump told me when I cut out the bunny for the Easter picture. I was cutting so carefully and then I made the wrong mistake."

"You don't make the wrong mistake," said Billy. "You just make a mistake."

"I know," said Emma. "Like when you were stupid and didn't ask one question."

"I've got a great idea!" said Mr. Reynolds.

"What?" said Billy.

"It's a surprise."

"A naked mole rat?" said Emma.

"Something better," said Mr. Reynolds.

"I doubt it," said Emma.

Mr. Reynolds put down his sandwich and went to find a phone.

Rodeo

That night Billy had a talk with Zucchini. They went for a walk behind the Holiday Inn, Billy holding Zucchini's leash, Zucchini sniffing about the close-cropped grass and occasional bushes.

"I'm sorry I couldn't take you to the prairie today," said Billy.

What's wrong? Zucchini wondered. Why couldn't you take me?

Billy sat down on the grass and held Zucchini close. "I wanted to take you," he said, "but there was a reason I couldn't. I can't explain it now, but I will. I'll take you. I promise. You have to be patient."

Everyone's telling me to be patient, thought Zucchini. First One-Day Service, and now Billy. It's not easy to do. I hope I get some patience soon.

After dinner they went to the rodeo. Zucchini had a great time. He sat on Billy's shoulders and watched as clowns in brightly colored costumes distracted giant bulls who went charging around the ring, heads down and snorting.

This is exciting! thought Zucchini.

He watched the cowboys rope calves, wrestle steer, and ride the bucking broncos. Then came the barrel racing. The first rider was a five-year-old girl. Her enormous black horse charged out of the starting gate, its tiny rider kicking with short legs. The girl's boots were bright flashes of red in the spotlight shining down from the judges' tower.

"That's for me," said Emma. She stood up on the narrow plank of the bleachers.

Mr. Reynolds grabbed her by the seat of her kangaroo suit. "Nothing doing," he said.

"But why?"

"Sit down."

Emma sat. Her lower lip began to tremble. Eyes wide, she watched the girl kick furiously and flap her elbows as her horse sped around the barrel in a tight circle, then took off across the arena.

The sun was setting behind the mountains as Zucchini watched from his perch, the cool evening breeze blowing in his face.

This is great, he thought. I'll worry about getting patience tomorrow.

In the morning they left for the Teton Mountains. Their next stop was Jackson Hole, where Tom Campbell had his research company. Billy had a lot to ask Mr. Campbell about the survival of the black-footed ferrets. He hoped he had the courage.

Maybe I'll hear from Miss Pickett when I get to Jackson Hole, he thought as they headed west on Route 14. Maybe she'll say she made a mistake, that Zucchini is a domestic ferret after all. Then I can keep him! I have to!

Zucchini took his position on Billy's shoulders. He pressed his nose against the glass and peered through the window as they passed through Shoshone National Forest.

The rust-red clay buttes rose like towers to the sky, the gentle river wound below, and all around Zucchini saw the pine trees, the sagebrush, and the aspens, feather soft, with the snow-capped mountains high in the distance.

Soon they entered Yellowstone Park, the home of wolves. Billy had followed the debate on returning the wolves to their land. He felt they belonged there. He thought of Margaret, the girl from next door who loved them so. Billy didn't see any wolves that day, but he saw nineteen buffalo, two elk, seven moose, a herd of antelope, five deer, and a golden eagle.

Heading south, they entered Grand Teton National Park. The giant Teton Mountains went straight up from the gentle valley. Billy loved the soft forest beds, the glaciers, the lakes, the meadows high up, the tall pine trees, and the aspens with their white trunks. The mountains were mostly covered with snow, but near the bottom their slopes were clear, a good place for mountain sheep to graze.

When they reached Jackson Hole, they drove up a long winding road to the top of a butte. Here they stopped at Spring Brook Ranch, a resort with small wooden cabins along the rim of the butte. From their room they had a view of the whole valley. Billy stood at the window, holding Zucchini as they looked across the valley, past the cows, to the Teton Mountains rising without warning straight up from the valley floor. The peaks of the mountains were jagged and white like the teeth of a shark. Zucchini could hear the sound of his heart beating. He felt very small.

Tom Campbell

The next morning the surprise came. Zucchini watched from inside his sweatshirt sleeve as Billy opened the package. It was a tape recorder. Mr. Reynolds had called Billy's stepfather and had asked him to send it from his audio-equipment store by overnight mail.

"Thank you," said Billy when he saw the shiny black machine. It was not much bigger than a deck of cards.

"Now here's the thing," said Mr. Reynolds. He had woken up hungry and was eating cashew nuts and drinking V-8 juice from a can as he spoke. "You can use it for your interviews. You write out your questions before you go. Then when you meet the guys, you read the questions and tape their answers."

"They might be girls," said Emma. She was watching TV and spoke without turning around.

"They're not," said Billy.

"Girls can answer questions."

"I know," said Billy.

"And lots of girls know about ferrets."

"Women study ferrets," said Billy, "but the people I'm trying to interview right now are men."

"Maybe not."

"Their names are Tom."

"My friend's name is Sam and she's a girl."

"These are guys," said Mr. Reynolds.

"Maybe not," said Emma. "Everybody thinks it's boys and the girls get shuffled back."

"You're not going to get shuffled back," said Mr. Reynolds. "I wouldn't worry about it."

"Some girls do," said Emma. "They think it's only boys who can be it and they don't try."

Mr. Reynolds finished off his V-8 juice. He threw the can into the wastebasket on the far side of the room. "I'm glad you don't think that way," he said.

"I don't," said Emma. "Girls can be anything. Like horse riders or truck-driving people or garbagemen too if they want."

"Of course they can," said Mr. Reynolds.

"Garbagewomen," said Billy.

Mr. Reynolds picked up the tape recorder. "So here's what you do," he continued to Billy. "You ask the people—"

"That's better," said Emma.

"You're right," said Mr. Reynolds. "You ask the people if it's all right to tape the interview, and if they say yes, you're in business."

"Can I try it?" Emma asked.

"Maybe later," said Billy.

"Kangaroos like tape recorders. They keep them in their pouches."

"Not this one," said Billy.

Before they went to breakfast, Billy called his mother. She had heard nothing from Miss Pickett. Billy was disappointed. He tried not to worry, but it was hard. It was also hard to call Tom Campbell, but he had to. They had come too far to stop now.

"Biota," said the friendly voice on the other end of the phone.

"Is Tom Campbell there?" asked Billy.

"This is he."

Billy took a deep breath. He had written out what he wanted to say on a small piece of paper. "My name is Billy Reynolds," he read. "I'm studying ferrets for school. I wanted to meet you because I need to ask you questions."

"That'd be fine," said Mr. Campbell.

"When can I ask you the questions?"

"I have some time today," said Mr. Campbell. "Want to come by at noon?"

"O.K." said Billy. He wrote down the directions very carefully, said good-bye to Mr. Campbell, and hung up the phone.

I did it! he thought. That wasn't so bad.

Zucchini watched from his cage inside the Pathfinder as Billy, Mr. Reynolds, and Emma walked toward the wood-beam house. Billy knocked on the door. A nice-looking man in jeans and a long-sleeved polo shirt with small letters on the upper left side opened the door.

Who's that? thought Zucchini.

It was Tom Campbell.

Billy's heart raced with excitement as they went inside the house.

"You must be Billy," said Mr. Campbell, closing the door behind them. "It's good to meet you."

"My tooth is bent over from looseness," said Emma. "Want to see?"

"Well, sure," said Mr. Campbell.

"Not now," said Mr. Reynolds. "Billy needs to talk with Mr. Campbell. We'll leave them alone for a while."

Billy felt a wave of panic. The idea of being alone with a famous biologist was scary. He told himself to calm down.

This is what I came for, he thought. I can't stop now.

They arranged for Billy to be picked up in an hour. Then Mr. Reynolds and Emma left.

"Have a seat," said Mr. Campbell. He motioned to the couch by the window.

"Thank you," said Billy. He looked about the room. It had a cozy feeling, with lots of light. There were plants, and pictures of wildlife, and lots of books. A map of a riverbed hung near the door to the kitchen. Below that, in a cabinet, was a collection of small animal bones.

Mr. Campbell sat across from Billy. Billy liked him right away. He was tall, with a friendly face and light-brown hair. He wore the same kind of sneakers Billy did.

We're alike, thought Billy. We care about animals and helping nature and we have the same kind of sneakers.

Billy felt in that moment that he not only admired Tom Campbell, but that he wanted to be exactly like him.

"So you're interested in ferrets," said Mr. Campbell.

"Yes," said Billy. He looked down at his tape recorder, which he held tightly on his lap, along with his list of questions.

"I see you have a tape recorder," said Mr. Campbell.

"Yes," said Billy. He appreciated the way Mr. Campbell spoke to him, as one person to another, not like he was speaking to a child. Then Billy remembered his plan. He took a deep breath and opened his list of questions. "Is it O.K. if I turn on my tape recorder?" he read.

"Sure thing," said Mr. Campbell.

Billy pushed the button that said RECORD.

"What got you interested in ferrets?" Mr. Campbell asked.

Billy thought of Zucchini. He wanted to tell Mr. Campbell all about him: how he had found Zucchini at the ASPCA; how he had built him a cage; how Zucchini liked the insides of lima beans; how he hid things under the refrigerator and walked on a leash and rode in Billy's sweatshirt hood; how he looked like a black-footed ferret; how he might even be one!

I can't tell Mr. Campbell yet, Billy thought. He would ask to see Zucchini. He would know if Zucchini was a black-footed ferret. If he is, I won't be able to keep him! I have to wait. Maybe I'll hear from Miss Pickett. Maybe she'll say he's a domestic ferret. Maybe she changed her mind. Maybe I heard her wrong.

He looked at Mr. Campbell. "I've been interested in ferrets for a long time," he said. "I saw one in New York and I liked it."

The Interview

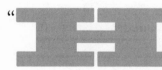"ow do you look for ferrets?" asked Billy. It was Question Number One on his list.

Mr. Campbell threw his leg over the side of his chair. "There's two ways you look for ferrets," he said. "It depends on the time of year. In winter you work in the daylight, counting prairie-dog burrows and tracking the ferrets in the snow. In summer you look for them at night with spotlights."

Billy looked down at his list. He was so excited. He could hardly believe he was really there, interviewing Tom Campbell! He breathed in deep, then read the next question.

"Where do you sleep?"

"You sleep in tents, or sheepherder's wagons, or sometimes in a house or a motel."

"That sounds like fun," said Billy. He surprised himself. He hadn't expected to say anything that wasn't on his list.

"It is," said Mr. Campbell, "but sometimes it's hard to sleep, especially if you're in a tent in bright daylight and you're sweating because it's eighty-five degrees out."

I wouldn't care about sleeping, Billy thought. I would be too excited.

He read the next question. "If some big company wants to drill for oil or put down a pipeline, can they do it even if it will hurt ferrets?"

"Companies have to have surveys done anytime they want to do something like that," said Mr. Campbell. "We have to be sure that what the companies want to do won't be bad for ferrets. It's the same with any endangered species."

The more Billy heard about Tom Campbell's work, the more he wanted to do it.

"Would you like some orange juice?" asked Mr. Campbell.

"Sure," said Billy.

"Hold on a minute." Mr. Campbell got up and went into the kitchen. Billy noticed how tall he was and how strong.

I want to be just like him, Billy thought.

And then he had another thought: I want to *be* him.

"Here you go," said Mr. Campbell. He handed Billy a tall glass of orange juice, then sat back down with a glass of his own.

"Do you think there are any more ferrets?" asked Billy. It was a question farther down on his list, but it came to his mind so he asked it then.

"I've become less optimistic over the years," said Mr. Campbell. He took a long drink of orange juice.

"What does optimistic mean?" asked Billy.

"Expecting the best," said Mr. Campbell.

"The best would be more ferrets?"

"Right," said Mr. Campbell. "I'd love to be wrong on this one, but I don't think they're out there. There's been a lot of people looking. The public is involved now. There's a ten-thousand dollar reward for anyone finding a black-footed ferret."

Billy thought of Zucchini. If Zucchini was a black-footed ferret, he would be worth $10,000!

That's a lot of money, thought Billy, but I don't care. I'd rather have Zucchini than all the money in the world.

He checked his list. "What else do you do with ferrets?" he asked. He could feel his shyness slipping away.

"Well, let's see," said Mr. Campbell. "We do surveys. We look for reintroduction sites."

"How do you do that?"

"We generally sweep through an area on foot. There's several things we look for. First, we collect burrow density information and plug that into our H.S.I."

"What's that?"

"Habitat Suitability Index. It tells us how good the

prairie-dog complex is for ferrets. If you're free one summer, you should come out with us."

"Really?" said Billy. He could hardly believe what he had heard.

"Sure," said Mr. Campbell. "I like to encourage future biologists."

Billy's heart was pounding. It sounded too good to be true. He put down his notes. New questions poured into his mind. He felt no fear. "What did it feel like after you found the ferrets in Meeteetse and then they started to disappear, but you didn't know why?"

"It was disturbing," said Mr. Campbell. "We should have moved them, but there was a difference of opinion. By the following summer, distemper had nearly knocked them out."

"I know," said Billy.

Mr. Campbell drank some more of his juice. "When you're dealing with an endangered species, you can't be too careful," he said. "Once a species is lost, it's lost forever."

"I know," said Billy. "They say ferrets don't matter, or owls, or eagles, but who knows?" There was no stopping now. Billy had to say this. He had thought about it for a long time. He cared so much. "I think everything is connected to everything else," he said. "One thing needs another thing and that thing needs something else. You can ruin something and then it's gone, like a kind of an animal, or certain trees, or rivers, or a small part of the atmosphere, but it could be a very important part. I think everything is important, only sometimes we don't know how. After it's gone, we could find out why the world needed it, but then it would be too late. We could never get it back."

Mr. Campbell set down his empty juice glass. He looked at Billy, but he didn't speak.

I said too much, Billy thought. I sounded stupid.

Mr. Campbell kept looking at Billy. He smiled. At last he spoke. "Anytime you want to come out with us," he said, "you just let me know."

Patience

They ate lunch at Nora's Fish Creek Café, a restaurant in a log cabin specializing in thick pancakes. Billy told his father all about the interview, how he had asked a lot of questions, how he had stopped being shy. "It just happened," he said. "Mr. Campbell was so nice and I was thinking about the ferrets. I forgot everything else."

"That's great," said Mr. Reynolds, cutting into his triple-decker stack of buckwheat pancakes. "I'm proud of you."

"My tooth is hanging by a thread," said Emma.

Billy ignored Emma's remark. "He said I could go on a survey," he continued. "He said I could help."

"It might even come out in my soup."

"I'll pull it out if you want me to," said Mr. Reynolds.

"No thank you," said Emma. "I don't want to encourage it."

"It won't hurt."

"They all say that."

"I wish I could have shown him Zucchini," said Billy.

"Why couldn't you?" asked Emma.

"It's complicated."

"Like my tooth. If I eat solid food, I might swallow it, my tooth, that is, which I don't want, because a tooth in my stomach is too strange to think of, but if I don't eat solid food, I might get weak and faint and hit my head on the floor and break my head bone."

When they went to pay their check, Billy noticed the large wooden fish hanging above the cash register. Its nose pointed downward and it held a dollar bill in its mouth. PAY HERE, it said in green letters on the side of the fish. Next to the register was a stack of postcards. The card on top showed a gray wolf standing alone on a rock. Billy thought of Margaret.

She'd like that postcard, Billy thought.

He decided to buy it for her. As he paid the woman behind the register (and under the fish), he had the thought that normally he wouldn't have bought the card. He would have wanted to, but he would have been afraid.

Maybe she already has it, he would have thought. Or maybe she has a better one. She'll think I'm stupid. Why should I give her a present? It's not her birthday.

These were the thoughts he would have had, but it was different now. Somehow, after losing his shyness in the interview, it seemed still to be gone. He decided not to mail the card, but to take it back and give it to her. He wanted to see her face when she looked at it.

Outside, Zucchini was waiting with One-Day Service in

the back of the Pathfinder. Once again the mouse was treading her wheel.

Patience, thought Zucchini as he huddled deep within his
sweatshirt sleeve. That's what I need. Either patience or a
pair of tiny earplugs.

Squeak, squeak, rattle, rattle, bang, bang, went the wheel.

"Smell the cheese, find the cheese, eat the cheese," said
the mouse.

Zucchini curled up in a tight ball, turning his head upside
down and tucking in his paws.

Earplugs would be nice, he thought, but they wouldn't
solve everything. I still wouldn't be on the prairie. Why won't
Billy take me? He said he would. I have to be patient. He
always keeps his word.

The next morning they left for Laramie. There was still
no word from Miss Pickett, and Billy was getting worried.

"You're awfully quiet," said his father as they headed
south on Route 191.

I was thinking that too, thought Zucchini.

He was resting on Billy's shoulders in his traveling position. He could sense Billy's worry.

"Will I ever see Buck E. Benson?" asked Emma from her
place in the back seat. "That's the question."

"No it's not," said Billy. He wasn't in the mood for
Emma's problems.

"It is to me," said Emma. "Everybody has a question, and
that's mine."

It's not a very serious one, thought Billy. It's not like wondering if you'll have to give away your best friend and never
see him again and never be able to explain.

That troubled Billy more than anything else, the idea that Zucchini might have to be sent away and never know the reason why.

Billy reached up, took Zucchini off his shoulders, and held him close against his heart.

Hamster Host

wo hours later Emma screamed.

"Don't scream," said Mr. Reynolds.

Emma screamed again.

I wish she wouldn't do that, thought Zucchini. He had been asleep on Billy's lap, dreaming of the prairie. He had been running in the grass, flipping in circles, rolling like a doughnut, sprouting wings.

"There he is!" shrieked Emma. She was jumping up and down in the backseat.

"Who?" asked Mr. Reynolds.

Billy didn't have to ask.

Zucchini peered through the windshield at the redbrick building with the white trim around the windows. Across the front of the building, just below the roof, was a large sign. BUCK E. BENSON'S BURGER ROOM PLAYSHOW, it said. Below the sign, shaking hands with a group of children, was an enormous hamster.

Who's that? thought Zucchini.

"Buck E.!" shrieked Emma.

"Don't scream!" said Mr. Reynolds.

"Turn here," said Emma.

Billy knew they would have to stop. They would have to shake hands with Buck E. Benson and play stupid games and eat burgers. Anything else was unthinkable.

Zucchini stared at the giant hamster.

I don't trust him, he thought as they pulled into the parking lot. He's too big, and he has hands.

"You have to stay here," said Billy, putting Zucchini into his traveling cage in the back of the Pathfinder.

For once Zucchini didn't mind.

Emma suddenly became shy. It was the first time Billy had ever seen her like that. She held her father's hand and hung back behind him, looking at the ground.

"Come on," said Mr. Reynolds. "You've been waiting weeks for this."

"I know," said Emma, still looking at the ground.

"Let's go," said her father.

"He's big."

"You knew he was going to be big."

"Not so much."

"Well, that's the size he is."

"Hello there," said the giant hamster. He was brown and furry with a fat belly, large teeth, and a polka-dot bow tie. He looked down at Emma. "You must be a kangaroo."

Emma stared at her boots.

"Well, my gosh," said Buck E. "We never had a kangaroo at the Burger Room before."

"I know," said Emma. She looked up briefly at the giant hamster, then back down at her boots.

"What do you have in your pouch?"

"Three pretzels and a rubber chicken."

"Well, what do you know." Buck E. pulled his furry sleeve away from his furry glove and checked his watch. "You should go on into the Burger Room and have yourself a good time."

"Say good-bye to Buck E.," said Mr. Reynolds.

"Good-bye," said Emma as they started through the door. "My tooth is hanging by a thread."

"Well, what do you know," said Buck E.

"Soon it's coming out," Emma called back over her shoulder, but the door had already closed.

Inside, Billy looked for a phone. He passed the burger stand and moved toward the game area. There was a line in front of a cagelike space surrounded by netting. Inside children jumped on an air mattress amidst many colored balls. At the end of the room was a stage where stuffed animals moved stiffly and sang a medley of songs about themselves.

Emma headed for the jumping-ball cage as Billy spotted a phone. He reached his mother right away, but the news was not good. Since she hadn't received the letter, Mrs. Ferguson had called Miss Pickett at the ASPCA. Miss Pickett was away on vacation.

The next day in Laramie, Billy put Zucchini into the tub at the Holiday Inn. He also put in his litter tray, his sweat-shirt sleeve, his food, and his water bowl. He thought the tub would be a nice change for Zucchini. He had to leave him alone for several hours.

"I have to leave you here for a while," said Billy. "I wish I could take you, but I can't."

Why not? thought Zucchini.

"Good-bye," said Billy.

Good-bye, thought the tiny ferret. Hurry back.

Billy left the bathroom, closing the door behind him. He hated to leave Zucchini, but he had no choice. They were going to the captive-breeding center. Dr. Thorne might be there. If he saw Zucchini, he might say he was a black-footed ferret, that Billy couldn't keep him. Billy had one more day in Wyoming, one more chance to hear from Miss Pickett. If he didn't hear by the afternoon, he would show Zucchini to Dr. Thorne. He would have to. But not a moment before.

What should I do? thought Zucchini as he sat in the large, slippery tub. Should I escape to the prairie alone, or should I try to be patient and wait? If I go alone, I might get lost. I might never see Billy again. I couldn't stand that. He said he would take me. But what if something happens and he can't? I have to get back to the prairie! It's the most wonderful place in the world!

Sybille

The Sybille Research Center was located in a beautiful canyon. Hills rose sharply on either side of the simple one-story buildings and outdoor pens. Many kinds of animals were studied and cared for at the center. Billy wanted to see them all.

Dr. Thorne was not due to arrive until after eleven. Billy had spoken to one of his assistants on the phone. The assistant's name was Ted, and he had offered to show Billy around.

Ted was outside when they drove up. He wore a red shirt and blue jeans and large lace-up workboots. After saying hello, he spoke about the ferrets. "We keep the ferrets in there," he said, pointing to the single-story gray-green building on the left. There was a sign out in front.

FERRETS

BREEDING

Quiet Please

said the sign.

"Maybe Dr. Thorne'll let you see 'em," said Ted.

I hope so, thought Billy.

"My tooth came out and there's a hole," said Emma. "I can push my tongue through."

Ted didn't seem to know what to say to that. He mumbled something unclear as he led them in the direction of the pens. "This here's your Rocky Mountain bighorn sheep," he said, stopping by the first pen. The area inside slanted sharply up a hill. Three sheep shared the space. They were large, with thick coats, and horns that curled in a half spiral. Two were standing, looking off into the distance, while the third bashed its head repeatedly into a large tree.

"Why is it doing that?" asked Mr. Reynolds.

"That's what they do," said Ted.

Billy had read about the bighorn sheep. He knew about their shockproof skulls.

Zucchini would like to see this, he thought. I wish he were here.

Ted showed them many animals—moose, deer, elk, and antelope. He showed them a mountain lion named Tanya and several snakes.

"Could I use your phone?" asked Mr. Reynolds when they reached the snakes. Snakes made him uneasy and he needed to call his agent. It seemed the perfect time to place the call.

"Over there," said Ted, pointing to a nearby door. He turned to Billy. "That's it besides the ferrets," he said as Mr. Reynolds headed for the phone.

Just then a man pulled up in a dark-green four-by-four. He hopped out and hurried over to where Billy and Emma were talking with Ted. He wore jeans and a tan short-sleeved knit shirt. He was drinking soda from a can. "Hi, there," he called out to Billy. "I'm Dr. Thorne."

"Hello," said Billy.

"You came a long way," said Dr. Thorne. "You must be pretty interested in ferrets."

"I am," said Billy.

"He has one," said Emma.

Billy felt as if the ground had opened beneath his feet.

"He's black-footed," Emma added.

"He's probably domestic," said Dr. Thorne. He turned to Billy. "Where'd you get him?" he asked.

"New York City," said Billy. He was having trouble getting a deep breath.

"He likes lima beans," said Emma, "but not the skins. He spits those under the couch."

"If he's from New York, he'd be a European ferret," said Dr. Thorne, ignoring Emma's announcement. "He'd be what they call domestic."

"He's black-footed," repeated Emma. "He has the black foot parts and the robber face and he's in the tub at the Holiday Inn."

Billy's heart was beating fast.

"Black-footed ferrets are found out west here, or they used to be," said Dr. Thorne. "There's none around anymore, except the ones we released."

Thank goodness! thought Billy. He doesn't believe her.

Frannie

M r. Reynolds and Emma left Billy at the research center with his tape recorder and his list of questions. Mr. Reynolds would be checking the hotel for messages. If Billy's mother had received a letter from Miss Pickett, Mr. Reynolds would call Billy at the center and let him know.

Dr. Thorne led Billy past the FERRETS BREEDING *Quiet Please* sign straight toward the double doors of the captive breeding center. There were signs on both the doors.

BLACK-FOOTED FERRET BUILDING

No

Unauthorized

Admittance

said one sign. The sign on the other door looked like this:

CAUTION

Black-Footed
Ferret
Crossing

Inside the doors was a small office area with a desk and bookshelves and a couple of chairs. At the far end to the right was a shower.

"This is a 'shower-in' facility," said Dr. Thorne, finishing off his soda. "We can't risk germs getting in."

Billy followed Dr. Thorne's instructions. He left his tape recorder on the desk, then showered, dried off, and moved into a small room on the far side of the shower. Here he put on one of the pairs of coveralls that were hanging on hooks along the wall. The coveralls were adult size and far too large. Billy had to roll the cuffs up many times to keep from tripping. After that he put on a pair of rubber thongs, which he took from a cardboard box by the door. The thongs were large as well. They were hard to keep on his feet, but Billy didn't mind. Soon he would see the black-footed ferrets.

Billy was ready. He opened the door and stepped into a

brightly lit room. Video monitors lined one wall. On each screen ferrets could be seen, sleeping, playing, resting, or eating in their individual nest boxes. Sitting at the video controls was the veterinarian in charge. She had dark hair and wore a red shirt. She turned around when she heard Billy come in. "Hi," she said. "Come on in."

Billy moved farther into the room. Charts hung on the wall listing the names of the ferrets, their breeding schedules, and their progress. Scarface, Dexter, Cody, Rocky, Frannie, Cora, Rebel—colored marking pens listed them all.

"Have a look," said the veterinarian at the video controls.

Billy approached the monitors.

"Here's a new litter," said the veterinarian. The screen in front of her showed a mother and four babies.

"How old are they?" asked Billy.

"Three days," said the veterinarian.

Billy didn't have his list, but the questions came easily. "How big were they when they were born?" he asked.

"Half the size of my thumb," said the veterinarian.

A moment later Dr. Thorne came in. He showed Billy the sheets listing what each ferret ate, the isolation room for the sick ferrets, and the surgery room. On the far side of the surgery room was a door. In the door there was a window. "Look through there," said Dr. Thorne.

Billy stood on tiptoe and peered through the glass. There were five rows of cages with lights above. Suddenly, up from the tunnel in the cage nearest to the window came a black-footed ferret.

"That's Frannie," said Dr. Thorne.

She stared at Billy with sharp, inquiring eyes. She looked exactly like Zucchini.

Later Billy and Dr. Thorne sat in the front office, drinking soda from cans. There had been no word from Miss Pickett. Billy's father had not called. Billy had waited as long as he could.

"What if somebody had one?" Billy spoke suddenly, blurting the question out.

"Had what?" asked Dr. Thorne.

"A black-footed ferret," said Billy. His heart was beating fast.

Dr. Thorne opened another can of soda. "It would be unlikely," he said, pulling the metal ring, then pushing the aluminum tab back into the can. "There just aren't any."

"What if somebody did?"

"We'd isolate it. We'd study it to be sure it was healthy."

Billy could feel his heart thundering behind his ribs. "Would you release it?" he asked.

Dr. Thorne shook his head. "We wouldn't know where it came from. We couldn't determine its effect on the breeding chain."

"Where would you put it?" asked Billy.

"We'd probably send it to a zoo."

"Oh," said Billy. Tears were beginning to press up behind his eyes. He took a deep breath. Then he spoke. "I might have one," he said. The minute he said it, he wished he hadn't. He felt his life would never be the same.

Dr. Thorne took a long sip of soda. "It's probably European," he said. "Domestic ferrets sometimes look like black-footed ferrets."

"I know," said Billy, "but mine has short hair and he's soft and his tail is only black at the tip."

"Have you got a picture?"

Billy took his wallet out of the back pocket of his jeans and took out his favorite picture. It was the one where he was holding Zucchini at the ASPCA.

Dr. Thorne studied the picture. "Sure looks like one," he said.

Billy felt as if he couldn't get enough air. Dr. Thorne looked up from the picture. "Where is he?" he asked.

"At the Holiday Inn," said Billy.

"I'd like to take a look at him."

Billy felt numb.

"Can you bring him by tomorrow?"

"O.K.," said Billy. He felt a giant wave of fear.

Choice

illy was thankful to find Zucchini waiting for him in the tub when he returned to the hotel. Although Billy had left the DO NOT DISTURB sign on the door, he had worried just the same that somehow he might have been let out.

You're back! thought Zucchini as he crawled out from inside his sweatshirt sleeve.

Billy moved to the tub. "We have to go somewhere," he said.

Where? thought Zucchini.

Billy was taking Zucchini to the prairie.

The late-afternoon sunlight slanted from just above the horizon to the west as Mr. Reynolds pulled the Pathfinder onto the rough prairie ground on the side of the road.

Zucchini was filled with excitement. He sat up on his hind legs on Billy's lap and peered through the window, straining at his leash.

We're here! he thought. We're really here!

Emma was asleep in the backseat.

"We'll wait in the car," said Mr. Reynolds. "I've got a script to read."

Let's go! thought Zucchini. Open up!

Billy opened the door. Holding Zucchini tight, he stepped to the ground, turned, and faced the open prairie.

At last! Zucchini thought. It's more beautiful than in my dreams!

Billy walked for several minutes holding Zucchini, silent. It had snowed the week before and there were still many patches of soft white snow. Billy's sneakers were soon wet through. His feet were cold.

Zucchini breathed in deep. He could see for miles in all directions. To the west were the mountains topped with snow. All was purple-pink in the glow of the afternoon sun.

When Billy reached a dry patch of prairie earth, he stopped. Then he sat down. He unhooked Zucchini's leash and took off his halter, but Zucchini didn't move. He sensed something in Billy that he couldn't understand. He sat at

Billy's side, staring into his eyes, searching for an answer.

After several moments Billy spoke. "I have to tell you something," he said. He cleared his throat. The dampness had made him hoarse. "There's a kind of ferret that's endangered," he began. "That means there's almost no more left. There's a lot of animals like that. People messed everything up. They poisoned nature and a lot of animals can't survive."

How awful, thought Zucchini.

"The ferrets that are endangered are called black-footed ferrets."

I have black feet, Zucchini thought.

It was as if Billy had read Zucchini's mind. "A lot of ferrets have black feet," he said, "but only a few of them are endangered. It's against the law to keep them if they are." He paused. He could hardly bring himself to continue. At last he spoke. "If you're endangered, I can't keep you."

Oh, no! Zucchini thought.

Billy forced himself to go on. "Tomorrow I'm supposed to take you to the research center. If the doctor says you're a black-footed ferret, I have to give you up."

Slowly Zucchini stepped into Billy's lap. He stood for a moment, confused and frightened. Then he lay down.

"I'm telling you this because I love you," said Billy. "I don't even know if you can understand."

I understand, thought Zucchini. I wish I didn't.

"You have a choice," Billy went on. "You can stay with me, or you can go free. You can stay on the prairie forever."

Without you?

Tears were burning Billy's face. He wiped them off with the sleeve of his jacket. "I can't stay with you," he said, "but at least you'll be free. If you come with me and you're endangered, they'll put you in a zoo. I couldn't stay with you there, either, and you'd be in a cage."

Zucchini lay in Billy's lap, limp and lifeless.

I don't want to leave you, he thought.

Billy looked across the prairie. He had brought Zucchini to a spot far from where the ferrets were being released. If Zucchini was a black-footed ferret, Billy didn't want him to disturb the breeding chain. He looked down at Zucchini, stroking the soft fur of his back. "You'd better go," he said. "It's the only way."

The sun was setting now. The wind was cold. After several minutes Billy set Zucchini on the ground. "Go on," he said. "You have a chance to be free."

Zucchini didn't move. He looked at the open range, the soft snow, the mountains in the purple light.

"Go on," said Billy.

Slowly Zucchini started off. After a few steps he stopped. He turned to look at Billy.

"Go on!" repeated Billy, louder this time.

Zucchini started walking. Ahead he could see the mountains. On he walked, because Billy had told him to go. He moved steadily ahead, the tiny animal in vast expanse of nature, moving slowly away from his friend.

Billy couldn't watch. He hung his head and closed his eyes as he sat silently, not moving, feeling completely alone.

I hope he makes it, he thought. Please, let him survive!

He wanted to call out, to stop Zucchini, to bring him back, but he didn't.

Let him go, he told himself. He needs his freedom.

Billy remained motionless, not breathing almost, as the minutes passed. There was no sound, not even the wind. Soon it was dark.

I should leave, he thought. I can't sit here forever.

And then it happened. A cold nose brushed against his hand.

New Tricks

n the way back to the hotel they stopped at Chuck's Ruff'um Up Steak House for dinner. Zucchini sat in his cage in the back of the Pathfinder next to One-Day Service, who was in her cage, running as usual on her wheel.

What will become of me? Zucchini wondered. Will I be special and live in a zoo? Will I be ordinary and stay with Billy? Please let me be ordinary! I want to stay with Billy forever! I'll even put up with One-Day Service. She's not so bad. She's small and scared and it makes her do strange things. I know how that can be. My life is good. When you get a bad shock, it makes you see how lucky you are.

Squeak, squeak, rattle, rattle, bang, bang, went the wheel. One-Day Service was running with a wide stride, body long, ears gently back.

Nothing stops her, thought Zucchini. She should deliver the mail.

Zucchini moved up to the edge of his cage and addressed the mouse. "I may be leaving," he said.

"Short cheese, long cheese, mild cheese, strong cheese," said the mouse, deep within a world of her own. She looked straight ahead through the orange plastic of her cage at the inside edge of the rear-window frame.

"I may not come back," said Zucchini.

The mouse stopped. "What?" she said. She steadied herself on the wheel, which shook from the sudden stopping.

"This may be my last night."

"What do you mean?" The mouse's pink eyes seemed to pop forward in their sockets.

"I might be endangered," said Zucchini. "People can't keep endangered animals."

"Are mice endangered?" asked the mouse.

"I don't think so," said Zucchini.

"Thank goodness," said the mouse. She climbed off her wheel and sat down in the middle of her cage. She stared at a nearby mound of wood shavings. "Where will you go?" she asked.

"It's not definite that I'm going," said Zucchini. "It's more or less a strong possibility."

"How strong?"

"I don't know," said Zucchini.

"If you do go somewhere, where will you go?"

"To a zoo."

"I hear most zoos are nice."

"Billy won't be there," said Zucchini.

"Neither will I," said the mouse.

Zucchini hadn't thought of that. It was a bright spot on a dark horizon.

"This is terrible," said the mouse. She was pacing now. She seemed upset.

"Why?" said Zucchini. "You never said you liked me."

"I don't talk a lot."

"You talk about cheese."

"You're a fine sort of animal," said the mouse. "You're large—"

"I'm not so large."

"You are to me. You're large and friendly and cheerful."

"Thank you," said Zucchini.

"You're welcome," said the mouse. "You're a comfort and a friend."

"Friends share things," said Zucchini. "We don't share anything."

"Maybe we could," said the mouse. "A mouse can learn new tricks."

"It's not a trick to be a friend."

"What is it?" One-Day Service moved closer, pressing her nose against the orange plastic wall of her cage.

"It's a constant sort of thing," said Zucchini. He thought about Billy. "It's listening and caring."

"I'll try it," said the mouse.

Zucchini was stunned at the depth of feeling within the tiny mouse. He stared at her through the bars of his cage, hunched and shivering behind the orange plastic. "I'm sorry," he said, "but I might have to go. There's nothing I can do about it. I wish there was."

Verdict

illy didn't sleep all night. His father tried to comfort him, but nothing worked. Billy spent the night sitting in the large chair by the window, holding Zucchini close.

This may be our last night together, he thought as he stroked Zucchini along his back.

Zucchini was thinking the same thing.

One-Day Service was quiet. Mr. Reynolds didn't even have to remove her wheel.

In the morning they loaded the Pathfinder for the long trip home. They would stop at the research center on their way. Billy lifted his duffel bag into the hatch in back. He was exhausted and felt as if he were moving through a dream.

"Turkeys are not smart," said Emma. She was dragging her suitcase toward the car. "Sometimes if they go out in the rain, they look up and open their mouths and they drown."

"What made you think of that?" asked Mr. Reynolds.

"It's raining," said Emma as if that explained it.

When they arrived at the research center, Dr. Thorne ran up to the car. It was raining hard, but he wasn't wearing a hat. "Bring him in here," he said when Billy rolled down the window.

Who's that? thought Zucchini, looking up from his place on Billy's lap. Bring me in where?

Billy got out of the car and carried Zucchini toward a

small wooden building off to one side.

Where are we going? wondered Zucchini as Billy followed Dr. Thorne through the rain.

Dr. Thorne opened the door.

"We'll wait for you here," called Mr. Reynolds. "Don't worry. I'm sure it'll turn out fine."

Inside, Billy continued to feel as if he were moving through a dream. He felt numb and distant. Everything had a hollow feeling.

"Let's take a look," said Dr. Thorne. He took Zucchini from Billy and put him on a table.

There were two other doctors in the room, but they didn't say anything. They stood around the table looking at Zucchini. Dr. Thorne looked at Zucchini's face. He looked into his eyes. He opened his mouth. He looked at his teeth. He looked at his tongue. He felt the shape of his skull. He looked into his ears. He stroked his fur. He stretched out his tail. He looked at his legs. He looked at his paws. He turned him over and looked at his belly. He turned him right side up. He held him up with one hand and looked into his face again. He set him back on the table. He looked at his tail. He said something about his tail to the doctors who were watching.

Zucchini didn't like being looked at so closely, but Dr. Thorne was gentle, and for that Zucchini was grateful. He waited patiently for the examination to end.

To Billy it seemed an eternity. He could hear Dr. Thorne's words, but they sounded as if they were coming through the small end of a very long tunnel. Billy held on to the edge of the table for support. He felt farther and farther away, as if he was in the blackness of space where the air was thin, or maybe there wasn't any air at all.

"He's not a black-footed ferret."

Dr. Thorne's voice shot through the room like a bullet, breaking into Billy's dream, pulling him back.

"He sure looks like one, I'll tell ya," said Dr. Thorne. "The lightness in color, the hair length, the weight, the markings, the cranial structure, the teeth. He almost had me fooled, but he's domestic."

Thank goodness! thought Zucchini.

"The dark hair between the forelegs is the tip-off. Black-footed ferrets don't have that. And another thing. Your ferret doesn't have any whiskerlike hairs on the outside of the front legs. We've seen those hairs only on black-footed ferrets." Dr. Thorne handed Zucchini to Billy. "He's yours," he said. "You're out ten thousand dollars, but you've got yourself a ferret."

Home

ust outside Laramie, Mr. Reynolds stopped the Pathfinder. Billy took Zucchini onto the prairie and they ran. The rain had stopped, the sun was strong, the air was crisp and clear. Billy spread his arms out wide like an eagle. He felt

like he was soaring in soft blue space, past the clouds, through the clouds, the breeze in his face, the sun on his back, free. Zucchini ran at his side, veered off to circle, then spun around to return to Billy's side. It was like Zucchini's dream. He was one with everything and everything was good.

On the way out of Wyoming, One-Day Service returned to her wheel. Zucchini had not yet mentioned anything to her, but she could tell. Zucchini was back to stay. In relief and excitement she ran at top speed.

She's off again, Zucchini thought.

"There's an eagle's nest," said Billy, pointing high up into a far-off tree.

"Eagles are the smartest birds in town," said Emma. "They run the postal service."

"They do not," said Billy.

"Yes they do," said Emma. "They're the leaders in overnight correspondence."

Zucchini did a lot of thinking on the way home. Surely he was the luckiest ferret in all the world, even if he had to share his life with a noisy mouse.

The night they crossed back over the New York state line, Zucchini rested on Billy's shoulder, staring though the windshield of the Pathfinder. The headlights from an oncoming frozen-food delivery truck caused Zucchini to blink. He shifted his position, then felt Billy's hand stroke him gently on the top of his head.

Billy said I need to be patient, he thought. It should be easy to be patient with a mouse, but it's not. I don't want to share my space with her. But I have to! It's her space as much as mine.

It had started to rain. Zucchini watched the windshield wiper cross back and forth across the windshield, keeping its even rhythm.

Patience will help, he thought. If I get patience, it will be easier. And it's good practice. If I can share my space with One-Day Service, I can share it with anything!

They picked up Route 17, and soon they were home.

The first thing Billy's mother said after she told him how happy she was to see him was that Miss Pickett had called that very morning. She had just opened Billy's letter upon returning from her vacation. It was her opinion that Zucchini was a domestic ferret. At first she had thought he was a black-footed ferret, but further research had changed her mind. She would not have allowed Billy to take Zucchini if he had been an endangered animal. Although she knew Billy would have given him a good home, it would have been against the law.

Billy wrote a letter back to thank her.

Mr. Reynolds had to leave right away because he was starting another movie. Billy tried to be brave, but it was hard to see his father go. Emma cried and held on to him for a long time at the door before he left. Afterward Mr. Ferguson made her a cup of hot chocolate.

Billy's school report was a big success. He gave it in front of all three fifth-grade classes in the cafeteria. They pushed the tables to the side and set up rows of chairs. Billy put up a screen so he could show the slides he had taken, along with his talk. He was very nervous, but he put Zucchini up on his shoulder and walked out in front of the group.

The first slide was of the prairie in Meeteetse. "This is where they first found the ferrets," Billy began. His voice felt like it was catching in his throat.

Zucchini sensed Billy's nervousness and nudged him behind his ear. It made Billy think of how his pet had returned from the vastness of the prairie to stay at his side no matter what, how that same nose had nudged his hand to let him know. Billy was filled with thankfulness. His fear began to ease.

The next slide showed a prairie-dog hole. Billy told about Pitchfork Ranch, about Jack Turnell and seeing the prairie dog. He told about meeting Tom Campbell; about Dr. Thorne and Frannie; about Lucille's Café and about the dog who found the first ferret.

When the slide of the Tetons came on, Billy told about how every creature on earth is important just like the rivers and the forests and the trees and the air. He was still a little nervous, but it didn't seem to matter. He felt more excited than afraid.

"Some people think the earth is so big that nothing humans can do will have any effect," he went on. "I don't think that's true. I think everything is connected to everything else, and what we do changes the earth and the atmosphere a lot. I don't think nature can take whatever hurting things we do to it and just be fine. Nature is powerful, but it can't save humans from too many stupid mistakes. We can't decide what matters and what doesn't, because everything matters, even if we don't know how."

At this point Billy showed a group of slides one after the next: a pine tree; a moose; a sunset; Zucchini on the prairie; a waterfall; a rainbow; a buffalo; a meadow.

"It's not enough to teach kids in school to get good marks

and remember things," he continued. "We have to learn what to do with the stuff we learn and how to figure things out. We need new ideas because a lot of the old ones aren't working. We have to learn how to take care of living things and about the balance of nature and how we're pushing it too far. My trip to Wyoming taught me a lot about these things and I hope I can think up new ways to help the earth. The end."

A lot of the kids said they liked Billy's report. Margaret was the first one. She came over to him by the tables on the side of the room to tell him.

"Your talk was good," she said.

"Thank you," said Billy. Then he gave her the wolf post-card. She liked it.

Billy's teacher said his report was excellent. She told him she had an idea. If he thought it would be fun, she wanted to write to Defenders of Wildlife to see if they would like Billy to write a column for children in their magazine. Billy liked the idea.

I could find out about a lot of things and write about them, he thought.

Possibilities filled his mind. He could learn about how the biologists were training the ferrets for reintroduction; about how they were trying to save the peregrine falcon and the spotted owl and the wolf; he could go on a survey with Tom Campbell; maybe he could even go to Yale University and interview Tim Clark.

That afternoon Billy put Zucchini in the hood of his sweatshirt and took him to Oppermans Pond. It was a warm April day. Billy walked through the welcoming pine forest to the edge of the pond where the spring flowers were just coming up. He sat down on his favorite rock, lifted Zucchini out of his sweatshirt hood, and set him down at his side. Zucchini breathed in deep. The sunlight reflected off the pond, and all was still.

BARBARA DANA, an actress as well as an author, was born in New York City. She is the author of several previous novels for children and young adults, including *Zucchini*, the first book about Billy and his pet ferret. *Zucchini* received the 1984 Washington Irving Children's Book Choice Award, the 1986 Maud Hart Lovelace Award, and the Land of Enchantment Award for 1986–87. Her book *Necessary Parties*, for older readers, was a 1986 ALA Best Book for Young Adults and was later made into a successful television drama. Ms. Dana has appeared often on television and in several films and plays. *Young Joan*, her novel about the young Joan of Arc, grew out of her starring role in a production of *Joan of Lorraine*. She and her husband, actor-director-author Alan Arkin, live in Connecticut and Nova Scotia. They have three sons.

LYNETTE HEMMANT was born in London and spent her childhood in south Wales and Australia before returning to London. She went to art school at fifteen. After many years as an illustrator, she started etching, then painting landscapes. She particularly loves painting the English countryside and gardens but also works in Italy, often in Venice. With her husband and a cat, she lives in a two-hundred-ten-year-old house in southeast London.